CU00525700

DRY

PER JACOBSEN

HUMBLEBOOKS

Copyright © 2023
Per Jacobsen & HumbleBooks
First edition, 2023

Artwork: Per Jacobsen

ISBN (paperback): 978-87-94319-19-5
ISBN (hardback): 978-87-94319-20-1

This is a work of fiction.
Any resemblance to real people,
living or dead, is purely coincidental.

*This book is dedicated to those
who have walked through the darkness.*

*Especially to the ones who took the lead,
carrying the torch.*

OTHER BOOKS BY PER JACOBSEN

THE MANSION OF MIRRORS (2020)

STRUNG (2021)

STRUNG II: THE VALLEY OF DEATH (2022)

STRUNG III: THE LAST DROP (2022)

THE RUDE AWAKENING OF THEODOR MOODY (2023)

Dear reader,

Before we start, I want to warn you that this novel deals with topics that may be sensitive for some people. It touches on themes such as suicide and incurable disease, and while my reason for including such topics was quite different—to explore what my characters would do if I robbed them of all hope—I'm well aware that these topics can be painful for some people.

That's my cards on the table and now it's up to you to choose whether you want to continue reading. And if the answer is no, that's perfectly okay.

Are you still here? Great, then buckle up, because we're about to enter the tunnel—and there is no light at the end.

—Per Jacobsen

"Water can be a source of life,
as well as death.
Just like hope."

R. Morgan, The Flood

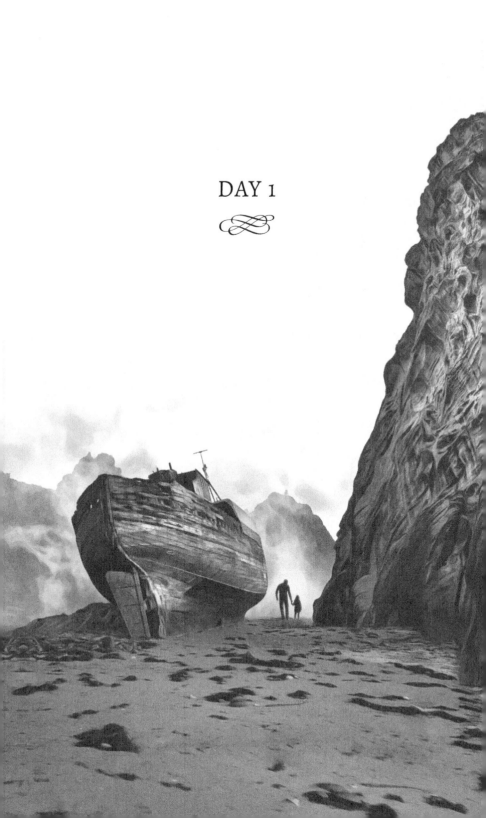

DAY 1

CHAPTER 1

"Both hands on the railing if you're gonna stand that close to the edge, sprout!"

"You promised you'd stop calling me that, Dad! And I need to be out here. Otherwise, I won't be able to see the reef when it shows up."

In addition to her words, Jessie wrinkles her nose in a *just-so-you-know* grimace. Her dad pretends not to see that, though. That's the reward for her hands —both of them—now having a safe grip on the ship's rail.

To be fair, it would also be a double standard if Nathan gave his daughter a hard time because of her interest in the sea and its inhabitants. After all, he has dedicated his life to it, working as a marine biologist for almost eight years.

Actually, this job is the reason why he and Jessie are standing here right now, on the deck of this small cargo ship bound for the Galapagos Islands. He's been tasked with documenting some cases of coral bleaching reported by locals and investigating whether the changes in water temperature are to blame. And Jessie? She came along hoping to fulfill a lifelong dream of seeing a sea turtle in the wild.

"You'll be standing there for a long time if it's the reef you're waiting for," he says, tousling the girl's auburn hair. "It doesn't start until a few miles from the coast, and right now we're at least fifty nautical miles away."

"Fifty what?"

"Nautical miles. That's how distances are measured on the water. They're a bit longer than regular miles, so ... around sixty miles, give or take."

"Sixty miles?" Jessie shoots her lower lip forward and lets out a sigh of despair. "Oh, man. It'll be dark before we get there."

"Hardly," Nathan laughs, then kisses her on the forehead. "It's only half past eleven in the morning, so I think we'll manage."

Jessie shrugs, placing both of her forearms on the top edge of the railing and leaning forward so that her chin rests on them.

"We could play some cards if you like?" Nathan tries. "Pass some time?"

"Nah, it's okay, Dad. I think I'll just stay here and look at the ocean."

This is one of them, Nathan thinks. *One of the moments Michelle warned you about where Jessie should be allowed to be alone with her thoughts and you should just leave her be.*

That's how he thinks—and yet he nudges her gently with his elbow.

"We could look upward instead. The weather is perfect for it."

She looks at him and then up to the sky, to which his index finger is pointing.

"Airy Tales?"

He nods, and she smiles.

A few minutes later, they're in the bow of the ship, both lying on their backs on top of the tarp covering one of the ship's life rafts.

The game is simple; Jessie spots shapes in the clouds, and her dad has to come up with a story that incorporates them all, to the best of his ability. Today it's no small task as the girl sees princesses, dragons, knights, and trolls up there ... as well as spaceships, parachutes, and a single dinosaur.

When she was younger, the stories were a means to get Jessie to sleep. Now it is often himself who succumbs to them. That is also the case today. While the troll opens the airlock and climbs into his spaceship, following the final boss battle against the evil knights of the periodic table, Nathan's eyelids turn heavy. His eyes blink, at first in time with the soft rocking from side to side of the deck, then slower and slower, until finally the clouds and blue skies above them disappear behind a blanket of darkness.

I can't keep doing this, Nathan. I won't keep doing this.

It's far from the first time these words have woken him up, only to keep echoing in the back of his mind after he opens his eyes—and he knows it won't be the last either. They are going to haunt him until the day when he closes his eyes for the last time. And he can only pray that it will at least stop there.

Today, however, Michelle's words don't get to torment him for long, as several other things rapidly steal his attention.

The first is the sky above him. It's no longer blue with scattered clusters of clouds. It's a pearly white. As if someone has covered it with a giant sheet. The second thing is the realization that he's alone on the tarp of the life raft. Jessie is gone.

He glances at his wristwatch, squints, shakes his hand, and looks again.

Quarter past twelve? That can't be right. Then he has only slept for ... what? Ten minutes?

"Jessie? Are you still here?"

No answer, not from Jessie or anyone else. In fact, it's so quiet on the deck that the sound of the plastic tarp crackling underneath him when he moves is all he can hear. And although this small cargo ship isn't as full of life as a cruise ship would've been, that's not normal. Usually, there are a few crew members up here, at the very least.

"Jessie?" he repeats as he pushes himself off the edge of the lifeboat and lands on deck. "If you're hiding, I need you to come out now."

Still nothing.

With an increasing unease in his stomach, he moves toward the middle of the ship, where the nearest staircase to the lower deck is located. He doesn't walk down it, though, because as he gets there, he spots Jessie's red hair. She has once again placed herself all the way out by the railing, this time at the stern. And she's not alone. Next to her are two other people who, like her, seem deeply preoccupied with something down in the water.

One is Earl Gibson. He's one of the two ship mechanics who help the chief engineer keep the ship's engine running.

Despite an intimidating exterior—a face filled

with deep, furrowed wrinkles, and rough hands, the nails of which are always black with oil and dirt— Earl is one of the friendliest crew members they've met on the trip. He even gave them a tour of his workplace down in the engine room when Jessie asked what his job was on the ship.

Judging by the object in his hand, though—a small, silvery hip flask—the good Mr. Gibson has apparently punched out for the day.

The other person is an elderly lady in a long, gray coat. All Nathan knows about her is that she boarded the ship in Manta Port, just like them, and that she isn't part of the regular crew either.

"What's so intriguing?" he asks, walking up behind them, and to his surprise, all three of them jump at the sound of his voice.

"Dad!" Jessie exclaims. She sounds strangely out of breath, as if she's been running. "You've gotta see this!"

"She's right," Earl agrees. "You're a marine biologist, right?"

Unsure if this is a question the mechanic actually wants answered, Nathan merely squints.

Earl's reply is also inarticulate. He just waves his hand—*come closer*—and nods toward the water.

Nathan walks over to the railing and grabs its

edge. Then he leans forward—and momentarily loses his ability to breathe.

The water is filled with bubbles. Thousands of them. Small, quivering bubbles that emerge on the surface, grow larger, and then burst.

"What is it?" he hears Earl whisper beside him. "A ... shoal of fish or something like that?"

"Hardly. No shoal of fish is *that* big."

To emphasize his argument, Nathan points to a random place farther out on the ocean, where the water's surface is also broken by bubbles. In fact, there are bubbles in all directions, as far as the eye can see. It looks as if the entire Pacific Ocean is boiling.

Except that we would have been steam-cooked by now if that was the case.

"A bucket," he says. "I need a bucket and a rope."

He hears the cold, commanding tone of his own voice, and for a moment, he expects the mechanic to tell him to shut the fuck up and go get it himself. But Earl doesn't protest. He just nods, takes a few steps backward, turns around, and then sprints in the direction of the stairs down to the lower deck.

"What is it, Dad?"

"Probably nothing," Nathan replies, ignoring the skeptical look the lady in the gray coat sends him behind Jessie's back. "A family of octopi having a party on the seabed, maybe. They're probably down there singing birthday songs right now. That's why it's bubbling up here."

Jessie rolls her eyes but still can't help letting out a giggle.

"Did you see when it started, sweetie?"

The girl shrugs and tilts her head at an angle.

"It had started when I came up here, about five minutes ago," says the elderly lady with the coat. She hesitates for a moment, glancing down at Jessie, then adds, "I, um ... noticed the girl and thought she was a bit young to be running around on deck unsupervised."

For a split second, a snide response burns on the tip of Nathan's tongue, but he chooses to swallow it and instead mumbles:

"And what about the fog? Did it appear at the same time?"

"I believe so ... but I don't think it's a fog."

Nathan opens his mouth, intending to ask what makes her say that, but right away, the answer comes to him on its own.

The air. It doesn't feel cold or damp. If the white blanket that has been pulled out across the blue sky while he slept were actually a fog, the air would be heavy and humid.

But it isn't. On the contrary, the wind feels bone dry when it hits his cheeks.

What the hell is going on?

The sound of quick footsteps on a metal grate makes him turn around. It's Earl. He's back, and he's brought a nylon rope and a bucket with him.

Nathan accepts both and nods at him. Next, he ties one end of the rope to the handle of the bucket and pulls on it a few times to make sure the knot holds.

Lifting the bucket over the edge and letting go, it once again strikes him how eerily quiet the ship is. Part of it is due to all four of them anxiously holding their breath as he starts lowering the bucket the thirty feet down to the water.

But it's not just that. There's something else too. He just can't put his finger on it.

An almost inaudible *'plop'* marks the bucket's meeting with the bubbling surface of the ocean, and a second later he feels a pull on the rope as it fills with water.

He begins to pull it back up, first with heavy, slow jerks, then faster and faster.

"Careful," the lady in the gray coat warns. "You don't want to burn your fingers if it's hot."

"It's not hot," Nathan replies—and when he sees Jessie's face contract in worry, he adds, "It looks like it's boiling, but it isn't. If it were, we wouldn't be standing here."

He's pretty sure that what he has just presented is an indisputable truth. Nevertheless, he can't stop his fingers from shaking slightly as he closes them around the handle of the bucket and lifts it back onto their side of the railing.

His logic held true. The handle isn't hot and neither are the contents of the bucket. The water is just as freezing as you'd expect it to be this far out on the Pacific Ocean.

But whether he should feel relieved by that observation, he doesn't quite know. Because if the water had been boiling, it would at least have explained why the surface of the water—including the one down in the bucket—is still sizzling and bubbling.

Some microscopic organisms, too small to be detected with the naked eye, that release oxygen into the water? If so, it would be the fastest spread he has ever witnessed.

"What the fucking hell is this crap?" Earl mutters, as Nathan tilts the bucket at an angle so he can look down into it as well.

Behind him, the old lady's eyes shoot open, look down at Jessie, and then back at Earl. She's clearly offended by his choice of words when there are children present.

Under normal circumstances, Nathan would've shared that view. Right now, though, Earl's words are a pretty good reflection of what is going through his own head.

"I don't know," he says, putting the half-full bucket down on the deck. "But I think we need to bring this to Captain Matthews' attention."

"I'll talk to him," Earl says, starting to turn around, but Nathan stops him by placing a hand on his shoulder.

"Only Matthews for now, okay?"

Earl lets a thoughtful gaze slide down to the bucket and from there out to the sea. Then he nods.

"That's probably a good idea."

While Earl makes his way to the bridge to talk to the captain, Nathan turns his attention back to his daughter.

"Listen, sprout. I'll have to stay here and talk for a while, so it might get a bit boring for you. Do you think you can find your way down to our cabin?"

"Dad!"

"Oh sorry, I did it again, didn't I?" he says, pretending to slap himself on the forehead. "Can you find our cabin on your own, Princess Jessie?"

"Of course ... *if* I can eat the rest of the M&Ms."

"Blackmail? You're too smart for a seven year old ... *sprout*. But okay, then."

"I can take her down there," the lady in the gray coat interjects, putting her hand on Jessie's shoulder and smiling at her. "I'm headed downstairs anyway, and I could use the company ... and a piece of chocolate."

She winks at Jessie, who responds with a smile and a nod.

"The girls are teaming up, huh?" Nathan laughs, holding his hands up defensively in front of him. "Fair enough, then. You can go with, um ...?"

"Meredith," the lady says.

"Meredith," Nathan repeats, nodding at her, after which he leans down and kisses Jessie on the forehead. "I'll be down as soon as I've talked to Captain Matthews."

The woman extends her elbow, and Jessie takes it. Then they turn their backs on her father and stroll arm in arm across the deck in the direction of the stairs, as if they were just two girlfriends on a shopping trip.

In the meantime, Nathan redirects his attention to the railing and the mystery that unfolds on the other side of it.

He's never been particularly fond of things he can't explain—which was one of the reasons that studying biology appealed to him—and on the list of inexplicable things he's faced in his life, this is quickly approaching the top spot.

The simmering and bubbling sea surface, the sudden, dry mist. None of it is ...

Something in the water somewhere to the right of the ship catches his attention. Something smooth and black which he registers out of the corner of his eye—and which his brain initially assumes is a large sea creature. A whale, perhaps.

But what breaks through the surface of the water isn't the back of a whale. It's the tip of a cliff—and to his horror, he discovers it's not the only one. In several places around the ship, there are large, menacing shadows just below the bubbling surface of the ocean. And it looks like they're growing bigger.

In the wake of that thought, another one follows, and he instinctively leans down and picks up the bucket from the deck.

"Oh God," he hears himself groan as he looks down into it, confirming his terrible premonition.

Not so much as a drop. The bucket is empty. The water has vanished ... just as it's vanishing on the other side of the railing right now.

CHAPTER 2

It does cross Nathan's mind, but only briefly, as he catches a glimpse of the wheelhouse before he runs down the stairs to the lower deck.

The thought of whether that should be where he was headed. Whether his first priority should be to pass on his discovery to Captain Matthews—thus increasing the chance that more people will walk away from the impending disaster with their lives intact.

But as with most such philosophical dilemmas, the answer is short and simple: Jessie is his daughter. His flesh and blood. None of the others are.

At the end of the stairs, Nathan steps out into a long corridor that both looks and smells like something from a spaceship in a dystopian science fiction movie. The walls are sheathed with metal plates. From these, thick pipes stick out at varying heights, making the already narrow hallway feel almost claustrophobically constricted—a fact that's only made worse by the thick stench of oil hanging in the air.

Combined with his growing panic, these things are disquieting, to say the least, and his desire to edge his way through the corridor is just as limited as the space. He just hasn't got any choice, given that this section of the ship is the quickest shortcut into the middle section, where the sleeping quarters and common rooms are located.

A shrill, metallic squeal sounds from the hinges as he pushes open the door at the end of the corridor and steps over the threshold.

The following hallway is wider and far more inviting. For one thing, there are carpets on the floor and colors on the walls, and furthermore, the sound of humming and banging from the pipes has been replaced with sixties music that someone has put on the stereo in the crew's common room further on.

He runs down the hallway and steers right at the first side aisle. Then he counts—one, two, three—doors until he stops in front of the one to their cabin.

"Jessie?" he says as he opens the door. "Are you in here?"

No one answers, and when he looks around, the room is empty. The bunks, the chairs, the little fold-out table; everything is exactly as they left it this morning.

And yes, the half-empty bag of M&Ms is still lying on the table next to the playing cards as well. Ergo, Jessie hasn't been here.

"Damn it!" he exclaims. "Damn it, damn it, d—"

"Dad?"

He turns around and is greeted by Jessie's face. She stares at him with wide-open, startled eyes. Behind her, the elderly woman, Meredith, does the same.

"S-sorry," he stammers. "I couldn't find you, and ... I guess I panicked."

Still with the same look of confusion in her eyes, Jessie raises her hands. In them, she holds a bag of mixed candy.

"We stopped at the vending machine. Meredith bought this for me. I told her she didn't have to, but she said that ..."

"It's okay, sweetie," Nathan says in a voice he can barely control. "But listen, we'll have to save the candy for later. Right now, you need to come with me upstairs again, okay?"

"But you said—"

"I know what I said," Nathan interrupts as he

enters the cabin and drags the suitcase with their clothes out from under one of the bunk beds. After rifling through it for a moment, he pulls up a sweater —the thickest he can find. Then he opens the narrow closet behind the door and grabs the two life jackets lying on the top shelf. He keeps the biggest one himself and hands the smaller one to Jessie along with the sweater.

"Put these on. The sweater first, the life jacket on top."

Jessie nods and does as she's told without saying anything. Except that her eyes are talking to him.

Dad, you're scaring me. That's what they're saying.

"What's going on?" Meredith asks from the doorway behind the girl.

Nathan meets her gaze, and for a moment, he doesn't know what to say. Whether he should say anything.

"After you left, I looked in the bucket again," he ends up saying, hoping that phrasing might go over Jessie's head. "It ... was empty."

"I'm not sure I'm following what you're saying," Meredith begins, but then she does, and her eyes are reduced to two tiny lines. "Are you saying that ..."

Nathan swallows and nods. He then places a hand on his daughter's back and leads her with him, edging past Meredith, who is still standing in the doorway with one hand clasped to the sill as if she were leaning on it so as not to lose her balance.

"W-wait," she says. "Where are you going?"

"The life rafts. If I'm right—"

He doesn't get any further before a deep rumble reverberates through the corridor and the floor beneath them suddenly starts tilting to the left. He instinctively reaches out his hands, grabs Jessie, and at the last second manages to get her moved in front of him so it's his back—and not her face—that collides with the wall.

The blow pushes the air out of his lungs, and although every cell in his body tells him he hasn't got time for it, he's forced to take a moment to catch his breath.

"Dad?"

"I'm okay, sweetie. Just need a bit of air."

Another sound, this time a dry hiss, like a cat warning a playful puppy to keep its nose to itself, emerges somewhere in the bow, and then the floor falls back into something resembling a horizontal position.

"We need to get out of here," Nathan says, grabbing his daughter's hand. It's cold and it's quivering, but there's no time to worry about that right now.

With Jessie at his side and Meredith on his heels, he runs back in the direction he came from, focusing on keeping a good pace while trying to suppress his growing panic.

It's no easy task—especially not when the fluorescent lamps on the ceiling above them start flickering as they edge their way through the narrow corridor with the metal walls.

"We're almost there," he says when he hears Meredith sigh and feels Jessie's grip tighten around his hand. "We just have to get up the stairs over there and then we'll be up on the deck. And I'm not going to let go of you, okay? No matter what happens, I'm not letting go."

Hardly has Nathan made that promise before it's almost broken, because the ship crashes into something that causes the entire hull to tilt sideways once more, and for a split second, he is dangerously close to losing his grip on her hand.

Above them, the fluorescent light flashes again, after which it goes out. And this time it doesn't come back.

"I'm scared, Dad."

"I know, sweetie, I know, but ... do you remember when we were on holiday in Kutztown and visited the Crystal Cave?"

"Uh-huh."

"There was a stretch where we had to find our way in the dark, remember? We have to do the same now. It's pretty cool, don't you think? Kind of like Indiana Jones."

"Yeah, um ... I guess."

He waits a moment, and when Jessie still hasn't added anything else, he takes a deep breath to gather courage and pulls her along.

Enveloped in a straitjacket of claustrophobia— and the sickening stench of diesel oil—he forces his feet to move forward and his free hand to touch the walls and the cold surfaces of the large metal pipes until his fingertips finally find the railing of the stairs.

The contrast to the darkness is stark, and daylight burns like acid in his eyes as he pushes open the door at the end of the stairs and steps out onto the deck. He has to blink several times to focus ... and a few times more to accept that what he sees isn't a hallucination.

"This can't be," he hears Meredith mutter behind him, but he's unable to answer her. Truth be told, he's incapable of anything but staring in disbelief.

Large rock formations, painted in shades of gray and black, rise above the ship. *Tower* above it. It's as if a gigantic hand, the hand of a *god*, has reached into the seabed, grabbed the bedrock, and pulled it upward, forming a circle of mountains around the ship with the same ease as a potter shapes a clay pot.

Except that Nathan knows it's the other way around. It's not the seabed that's moving up toward them. They're the ones moving downward as the water level drops.

As the water fucking disappears from the ocean.

"NATHAN!" someone shouts somewhere to their right, and when he turns toward the sound, he sees Earl running across the deck. "GET THEM TO THE LIFE RAFT! NOW!"

Nathan hears the words, but for some reason, his brain can't make sense of them. The mechanic might as well have spoken to him in a foreign language. It's only when Earl gets close enough for him to see the details on his face properly that he's able to break free from his state of shock.

Because the mechanic's weather-beaten face, usually ruddy, has lost all its color and faded to a disturbingly pale hue, resembling a shiny mask of wax. His gray eyes are full of confusion and fear so pure, so childlike, it shouldn't even be possible to see in the eyes of a grown man.

The same fear flares up in Nathan—and with it comes a surge of adrenaline. He bends down and picks up Jessie, then joins Earl and sprints across the deck in the direction of the raft on which they lay, just an hour ago, spotting cloud figures and telling airy tales.

"Where's Captain Matthews?" Nathan asks as they run.

"Still on the bridge," Earl replies, pointing over to the wheelhouse. "He had to stay in there. We, um ... we caught something on the sonar."

Earl hesitates for a moment, and Nathan sees his gaze slide down to Jessie. A gaze that contains a mixture of worry and compassion.

"The rest of us can't follow if you speak in code," Meredith says behind them. "What is a sonar?"

"It's like a radar," Earl explains. "A radar that, among other things, measures the distance down to the seabed. And right now, we're directly above a chasm. A *very* deep one."

As if to underline how menacing a picture the ship mechanic paints with these last words, a loudspeaker somewhere behind them starts emitting a deafening wail every few seconds. Shortly after, a new sound rises from the interior of the ship. A jarring chorus of panicked human voices.

"FIND SOMETHING TO GRAB ONTO!" Earl roars, but there is nothing within their nearest radius, not even for himself. So, when the bang comes and the hull starts tilting to the side, all four of them are tipped over and slide helplessly toward the middle of the ship's deck.

Jessie, still in her father's arms, screams in terror,

and Nathan pulls her to him, attempting to encase her so his body will act as a buffer.

A sharp, short-lived pain, like an electric shock, shoots through his back and neck as their slide is brought to an abrupt halt by the side wall of one of the four containers stacked in the center of the deck.

"Are you okay?" he asks, and when he feels Jessie's head nod against his chest, he turns his attention to the other two, who are also lying on the deck, moaning. "How about you guys?"

"A little banged up," Meredith groans. "But I'll live."

"Same here," Earl says, raising a thumb that shivers a bit too much to be convincing. "But it's too soon to celebrate. There's no guarantee it's over yet."

Nathan glances at him and then lets his gaze drift to the right and up along the deck, which now slopes over them at an angle of thirty degrees. Maybe more. Up there, along the edge, the railing runs, and if Earl is right—if the ship is about to tilt back in the opposite direction—it isn't unlikely that they will be thrown over it. And even if they aren't, the impact will probably be enough to break a few bones.

He locks his hands behind Jessie's back and whispers that everything will be okay. Then he closes his eyes and prepares to feel the pull in his stomach as the center of gravity shifts and the ship swings back.

The pull never comes. The cargo ship stays there, stuck in its sloping position, and their ticket to the world's worst turbo-slide is thankfully never redeemed.

"Is it over?" he hears Meredith say.

"For now," Earl replies, pushing himself up and signaling the others to follow suit.

Halfway walking, halfway climbing, they move down toward the left side of the ship's bow. The plan is to reach the railing so they can lean on it as they continue to the life raft.

Upon reaching the railing, however, they don't proceed right away. Instead, all four of them stop abruptly, gasping in unison.

What's in front of them is a view of sand dunes, scattered rock formations, and thousands of fish writhing in pain as the air chokes them. Behind them, all they see is the vast chasm that Earl said the sonar had picked up.

The chasm over which the entire rear half of the cargo ship hangs.

CHAPTER 3

"There's a lock buckle similar to this one on the other side," Earl says, pointing as they make their way to the life raft. "You open it by pulling up the bolt."

"I see it," Nathan confirms, after which he puts Jessie down on the deck and tells her to hold onto the railing while he removes the tarp covering the raft. Next, he grabs the locking bolt with both hands and pulls on it. The rubber raft breaks free of the railing and unfolds to double size.

"I don't get why you're so focused on that raft," Meredith says in a voice that reveals she's reaching the limit of what her psyche can handle at once. But judging by the sound of distressed voices starting to fill the deck behind them, she's not the only one who's getting there.

"Without water, there isn't much purpose in a life raft," Earl says. "You're right in that ... but we can still use it as a hoist to get down."

As if to emphasize his point, he turns the handle in a towing winch that's mounted on the railing and connected to a small, crane-like lifting mechanism via a steel wire.

At the end of the wire is a metal lock. From this run four nylon ropes, which are hooked to the edges of the raft to ensure that it stays horizontal when in the air.

When the ropes are fully stretched and the life raft is no longer in contact with the deck, Earl turns his attention back to Nathan.

"Time to get in the elevator."

Nathan looks at the raft, then at Jessie, then back at the raft, and suddenly the idea of climbing into it seems completely insane. However, his reservations immediately disappear when the cargo ship suddenly creaks ominously beneath them and the hull slides a bit farther in the direction of the abyss.

He holds out his hand to Jessie, but she doesn't accept it. In fact, she doesn't even seem to register it. Her focus is solely on the rubber raft, which her eyes, terrified and wide-open, follow as it swings slowly from side to side a few inches above the planks of the deck floor.

"Jessie?"

At first, nothing. Then a subdued: "I can't, Dad."

For a moment, the repressed crying in the girl's voice paralyzes Nathan, and he catches himself standing just as motionless as her. Frozen, without the faintest clue how to get either himself or her moving. But then his gaze slips past the railing, onto the uncovered seabed, which most of all looks like a gloomy lunar landscape.

"Of course, you can't," he says with a smile as he bends down and pretends to pick up an invisible object with both hands. "You can't go to an alien planet without your space helmet."

With a solemn expression on his face, he walks over to her and puts the invisible space helmet over her head. Jessie lets him do it—and as he puts on his own helmet, she squeezes her lips together and nods firmly.

And this time she accepts his hand.

Cautiously—but also aware that time is running out—he helps her and then Meredith into the raft. Then he looks at Earl.

"You just go ahead," the mechanic says, shaking his head. "I'll get a lift from one of the others. They're gonna have to drag it over here to get down anyway."

Nathan lets his gaze drift past Earl and down to the rear deck, where another group of people is in the process of detaching an inflatable raft from the railing. Their panic can be both seen and heard. And for good reason. Because Earl isn't wrong; they wouldn't achieve anything by lowering the life raft from over there, since that part of the ship is hanging over the ravine.

"Are you sure?"

"Just get your ass up to your daughter and stop wasting my time," Earl says in a voice that invites no negotiation.

Nathan nods, gets into the raft, makes eye contact with his daughter, and adjusts his invisible space helmet. Then he gives Earl a raised thumb.

"The entire world is holding its breath," Nathan says in a ceremonial tone, his gaze fixed on Jessie as Earl turns the handle of the hoist until they are above the height of the top edge of the railing, and then pushes the raft so it swings out over it. "The two world-famous astronauts, Jessie Bray and her father, Nathan, are ready in the spaceship. Any minute now, for the first time in history, man will set foot on the planet ...?"

He waves his hand in a circular motion, inviting Jessie to finish the sentence.

"O-Oceanus," she stammers as the raft begins moving downward in long, uneven jerks.

"Oceanus!" Nathan repeats enthusiastically. "Of

course! The only planet in the galaxy, apart from Earth, that houses Jessie Bray's favorite animal."

"The sea turtle?"

"Exactly," Nathan says, making a strenuous swallowing motion. "That's our mission, Jessie. We have to find a sea turtle."

CHAPTER 4

Upon the shaky, somewhat swaying landing of their bright yellow spaceship, Nathan is relieved to discover that their immediate surroundings mainly consist of sand and rocks. Of course, there are a few fish here and there, but the big, eerie pile of convulsing fish he saw earlier is some distance away.

Despite this one relief, it is still pretty terrifying to stand there, surrounded by dark rocks on a sandy bottom that half an hour ago was hidden beneath forty yards of seawater, but now is bone dry.

"DID YOU GET OFF OKAY?"

Nathan follows the sound of Earl's voice, looks up—and lets out a gasp when he sees how far up the railing is. And given that the ship is leaning toward this side, this is actually the shortest distance.

"YEAH, YOU CAN GO AHEAD AND PULL IT
BACK UP!"

Earl responds with a two-fingered salute and
then disappears out of sight behind the hoist. A few
seconds later, the steel wire starts to judder. This
time, however, their spaceship doesn't get off the
ground, because right then a deep rumble sounds
from the hull. And then the ship starts sliding
backward.

Further out over the edge of the abyss.

What follows is like a scene from a nightmare.
Panicked voices rise and mix together to form a
macabre chorus chanting a blend of desperate cries
for help and pointless profanities.

In front of their feet, the life raft starts moving
with the ship, as the steel wire from the hoist gets
stretched out and pulls it.

In the middle of the ship, another raft—probably
the one they saw someone release earlier—is hurled
over the railing.

Undoubtedly, this is a desperate attempt to use
it as a landing cushion. The problem is, however,
that the speed at which the cargo ship slides over
the edge is increasing dramatically, so the two
crew members who try their luck don't land
anywhere near the inflatable raft. Instead, they hit
a rock much farther ahead, giving them the same

fate as the sprawling fish. Although theirs is immediate.

Nathan grabs Jessie and presses her head against his life jacket to protect her from the sight. Behind him, he hears Meredith let out a series of short, stuttering gasps.

A second later, however, it's a new sound that steals his attention. A long hiss, like when the valve of a gas burner is opened. He looks up—and feels his stomach tighten, halfway in panic, halfway in hope.

The sound comes from the two life jackets that Earl has folded around the stretched-out steel wire between the hoist and the life raft to protect his arms while using it as an impromptu zipline.

At first, it seems to work as planned, but about halfway down, the wire starts to burn through the foam blocks inside the life jackets. Strips of fabric are ripped off, and a thin, dark gray snake of smoke arises.

Four, maybe five feet away from the ground, it gets too much for Earl. He lets out a roar, releases his grip, and plunges downward.

His legs hit the sand first, and although he tries to reduce the damage by continuing into a roll after landing, the crunching sound upon impact leaves no room for doubt. It wasn't just sand he landed on.

Earl roars again, this time in pain, but his screams are drowned out by the cries of the panicked crew still trapped on deck—and by the hull's relentless creaking and cracking, as the ship continues to slide backward until it's so far out over the ravine that its center of gravity shifts. Subsequently, it plummets, along with all the innocent souls on board, into the abyss.

A last, deafening bang, followed by a large cloud of sand, emerges from the depths as the cargo ship hits the ground. After that, everything falls quiet. Even Earl, still sitting on the sand, clutching his lower left leg, is as quiet as the grave.

The mechanic was injured in the fall. Badly, judging by the anguished expression on his face. Yet Nathan just stands there, motionless as a salt pillar, while he stares back and forth between Earl and the long, wide trail that the ship dug in the sandy ground before crashing down. The trail curves a bit in two places, making it resemble a dirt road or a river. Correction; a *dried-out* riverbed.

Nathan is aware of how irrelevant that observation is, how *futile* it is, but that doesn't change anything. He is no more able to control his thoughts right now than he would be able to breathe on the moon using his and Jessie's imaginary space helmets.

He jolts as something touches his arm. It's Meredith.

"He needs help," she says, nodding toward Earl.

Nathan nods as well, after which he gently grabs Jessie's arms that are still hugging him and loosens their grip.

"We've got an injured astronaut," he says, kneeling in front of her. "And he's probably a little scared. So, it's important that the rest of us are extra brave so Earl doesn't become more nervous. Do you think you can do that? Can you be brave for me? And for the mission?"

Jessie wipes her eyes and nods her head up and down.

"Good," Nathan says, pointing down toward the rubber raft that some of the other crew members threw overboard earlier. "Then you and Meredith will get an assignment together. In the raft, there is an emergency kit. You two need to go get that, okay? And if there's an emergency radio in the raft, you bring that too."

Jessie replies with a nod, as does Meredith when Nathan looks at her.

"Excellent. Then you best get moving, Astronaut Bray!"

With those words, Nathan gets up and sends them on their mission with a sweeping hand gesture. Then he runs over to Earl and squats down.

"How bad is it?"

It's a rhetorical question as Nathan can see that it's bad. One thing is the large, burgundy-red smudge that now adorns the bottom of the left leg of Earl's blue boiler suit. Another—far worse—thing is the object that sticks out through the fabric on the opposite side. A small, rust-brown metal tube that one doesn't need a doctorate to know is a bad thing to have embedded in your calf muscle.

"I'm not gonna lie," Earl groans. "It stings like hell."

"I can imagine. Listen, I'll have to roll up the fabric so I can have a better look at it. I'll be careful, okay?"

"Just get it over with."

Holy fucking shit!

These are the words that go through Nathan's head as the pant leg comes up far enough to expose the wound. What he says out loud is:

"A good cleaning and a bandage, and, um ... then it will be fine."

"Oh, is that so?" Earl says, putting on an expression that—if that's what it's meant to be—has to be one of the scariest smiles Nathan has ever seen. "Then why do you look like a zookeeper who just realized he forgot to close the gate into the lion's den, huh?"

The answer is simple: Nathan's tense facial expression is due to him being able to see something now that he couldn't before, namely that the rusty metal pipe is at least two inches longer than it appeared to be. And that most of it is buried in Earl's calf muscle.

"Let me have a look," Earl grunts, grabbing his foot so he can twist his leg slightly and see it for himself. "Oh, fuck. Can you ... can you get it out?"

"Give me a second to think," Nathan replies, after which he glances toward Jessie and Meredith. "How are we doing with that first-aid kit?"

"On our way!" Meredith shouts back. "We've found it. But there is no emergency radio in the raft."

"No, of course not," Earl drones. "I'd expect nothing less from Matthews. Damned cheap ass, always trying to save a buck at the expense of safety."

"Just be quick, okay?"

Meredith doesn't answer this last request from Nathan, but it isn't necessary either because a moment later, she's on her way back with the first-aid kit in one hand and Jessie in the other.

"Well then," Nathan says as he takes the box and opens its lid. "Let's see what we've got to work with."

Three out of the four things he was hoping to see are in there. All things considered, that's not too bad.

"Which one do you want first?" he asks, looking at Earl above the lid of the box. "The good or the bad news?"

Earl stares at him for a moment, his jaw moving as if he's chewing on a piece of gum. Then he wrinkles his nose.

"The good."

"We've got rubbing alcohol, bandage, and tape."

"I can hardly contain myself," Earl says dryly. "And the bad?"

"No anesthetics or painkillers."

"Nah, figures."

From Earl's sweaty face, Nathan's gaze slips over to Meredith. He doesn't ask his question out loud and doesn't need to. Meredith understands, and she immediately puts her arm around Jessie's shoulder. Then she leans down and whispers something that makes Jessie nod, after which they both turn around and walk back in the direction of the raft.

Meanwhile, Nathan turns his attention to Earl's injured leg. He knows what he has to do—and he also knows that he's not the one who's gonna feel the sting—yet he needs a moment to gather courage.

"I'll try to do it quickly," he says, gently grabbing the end of the tube with his thumb and forefinger.

"Just get it done."

Nathan nods and clears his throat before placing his other hand farther up on Earl's calf muscle to provide counter-pressure. Then he counts to three in his head.

And pulls.

CHAPTER 5

The effect of adrenaline is impressive. Not only does it enable people to push their bodies to the limit—and sometimes beyond—when the going gets tough. It also enables the brain to lock its focus on the most pressing problem and push all other concerns aside. No matter how big they may be.

From the moment he pulls the metal tube out of Earl's calf muscle in one quick jerk, this is exactly what happens in Nathan Bray's brain. The adrenaline makes him immune to the shock of the vast amount of blood that starts to flow out of the hole. It makes him deaf to Earl's cries of pain as the alcohol hits the wound, and subsequently, it enables his hands to work very quickly as they grab the bandage and wrap his leg.

But the adrenaline rush only has a certain duration, and once the effect wears off, reality awaits—along with the concerns that were set aside.

In this case, reality catches up with Nathan when he looks at his hands after putting the last piece of tape on the bandage and realizes that they're covered in blood.

No, that's not entirely true. It's the moment after, when he glances around, looking for some water to clean the blood off his hands, that it hits him again.

They're sitting on a dried-out seabed. There *is* no water.

"I don't know whether to say thank you or give you a slap," Earl groans, holding out his hand. "That shit didn't feel good, I tell you."

Nathan looks down at his own hand and then wipes his palm on his thigh. When that is done, he accepts Earl's hand and shakes it.

"Don't mention it. Do you think you can stand up? Walk?"

Earl lets out a resigned snort and shrugs.

"I wouldn't say no to a pair of crutches or a cane ... but I think I'll manage. Where you're planning to walk to, however, I don't know."

"The islands?" Nathan says, halfway asking, halfway declaring. "That's the closest, right?"

"Don't mean to piss on your parade, but did you

look around? The Pacific Ocean has turned into a freaking desert, and in case you haven't noticed, our group isn't exactly made up of professional athletes."

Nathan feels the urge to protest but finds no useful words to do it with. Because Earl is right. A ship mechanic with a leaky calf muscle, a girl of seven, and a scrawny, elderly lady who must be close to retirement age ... if she hasn't already reached it. Not exactly a Dream Team.

"But we can't just sit here," is the best response he can come up with. "We have to try. *I* have to try."

Earl draws in air through his nostrils and slowly exhales it again, looking up at the sky. Then he rubs his cheek and shifts his gaze back to Nathan.

"I'm sorry," he says. "It's just ... those were my colleagues on that ship. Good friends, many of them, and on top of this crap with my leg, it just ..."

"Don't worry about it," Nathan replies. "I get it."

"Having said that, though," Earl continues, "it doesn't change the fact that we're in a real shitty situation. Because we're far from the islands. *Very* far. And the measly food rations in the raft aren't going to keep us going for long. And that's not even the worst part."

Nathan knows very well what the ship mechanic is going to say next. Nevertheless, he feels his stomach clench as Earl picks up a handful of sand from the seabed and lets it fall out between his fingers in small, thin jets.

Like grains of sand in an hourglass.

"This is what we've got," he says. "Dry-ass sand and dry-ass rocks. Not a drop of water."

"How does something like that happen? What can make water disappear like that?"

It's a rhetorical question. One that Nathan does not expect an answer to. And he doesn't really get one either. What Earl gives him is a fairly accurate summary of the thought process he himself has already gone through.

"My first thought was an earthquake," Earl says. "A fissure in the bedrock or something like that. But for the crack to be big enough for that much water ... we would have felt it. Besides, it would probably have triggered a tsunami. But the water was calm, and it wouldn't explain the bubbles either. A volcanic eruption underground might do that, but then the water would be boiling, right? So, what then? North Korea or China testing some crazy new bomb? Or maybe aliens that are building swimming pools in their own galaxy?"

The last sentence, Nathan recognizes, is an attempt to be funny, probably in the hope of lightening the mood a bit. It doesn't make him smile, though. Because as far as explanations go, it feels just as plausible as the others. Perhaps even more so, as he has a disturbing—and fairly strong—feeling that it isn't just here in the area between Ecuador and the Galapagos Islands that the water has disappeared. And if that's the case, if it's a global phenomenon, the first two explanations can be taken off the table right away.

"Whatever the explanation is," Earl grunts, brushing grains of sand off his hands, "it doesn't make a damn difference to us whether we know it or not. We're fucked anyway."

"Matches in a storm," Nathan mutters, nodding.

"You're talking about matches?" says a woman's voice behind them.

"Not really," Nathan says, looking over at Meredith and Jessie, who have returned without him noticing. "We're just blowing off some steam. You found something more, I see."

"There was another bag in the raft," Meredith says, pointing to the ground between her and Jessie, where there is an orange-yellow sports bag. "There are some blankets, some food and water, and a bit of survival gear in it. Still no emergency radio, I'm afraid."

"No, that figures," Nathan sighs. "And I reckon none of you happen to have a phone, right? Mine is ... well, in our cabin."

He looks at Earl and Meredith—and isn't at all surprised to see them both shaking their heads.

"So not only are we stranded on the bed of the ocean, in the middle of nowhere, with nothing to navigate by. Somehow we have also managed to assemble a group of four people, none of whom have a phone on them."

"Just a sec," Earl exclaims, making an attempt to stand up. However, it only takes a moment for him to realize that he might have been a little too optimistic, so he sits back down, contorting his face in pain. "Can, um ... can I borrow the bag for a moment, Jessie? There's something I want to check."

"Oh, yeah, sure," Jessie says, carrying the bag over to him.

Earl smiles at her and then proceeds to study the strap of the bag. Halfway up, his fingers stop at a small zipper. He zips it open, takes something out— and then his smile grows.

"It's still a long shot," he says, looking at Nathan. "But at least now we have a chance of finding the right direction."

He reaches his hand over toward Nathan with the palm facing up. In it lies a small compass.

Nathan nods and smiles. Then he stands up, walks over to Jessie, and kisses her on the forehead.

"Great job, Astronaut Bray. Great job."

CHAPTER 6

About ten minutes later, the four members of the
unlikely group of survivors stand side by side, staring
at the rugged landscape to the southwest. Huge areas
of rocks and dried-out sand that look more and more
like a desert, broken only by dark gray, mountain-
like formations.

All four observers carry the same discouraged
expression in their eyes. Not that anyone would
blame them. It's bad enough that they're forced to
traverse this eerie landscape if they hope to reach the
archipelagos, but to even get that far, they'll have to
pass the very first obstacle, which looks like something taken out of a nightmare.

The shoal of fish. The one Nathan spotted earlier.
Thousands of fish lying scattered across the seabed

between two large rock formations ahead. The majority have stopped moving, but a few are still twitching and struggling to stay alive. It's heartbreaking and at the same time deeply frightening to see the lives of so many creatures ebbing away at once.

"Are you sure this is the only way?" Meredith asks.

"The alternative is to circle around one of the rocks," Earl replies, pointing. "It'll cost us time that we don't have. Besides, it's just fish."

"Did you hear that, sweetie?" Nathan says, looking down at Jessie, whose face is still grimacing in the same way that it does when her cruel father insists that she eat at least two of the broccoli bouquets on her plate. "It's just fish."

"I don't care. They're gross."

In reality, Nathan in no way disagrees with that view. He's just not sure that letting the girl in on that secret would solve anything. Therefore, he shrugs his shoulders instead and says:

"Guess we'd better pull on our anti-gravity boots and jump around them then. That way it's kind of like playing a game of *The Floor is Lava*."

Jessie stares at him quietly for a while, and he feels a brief fear that this could be the crucial moment when her childlike innocence suddenly disappears so she can no longer be distracted by her dad's silly games and lame, second-rate jokes.

But then a cautious smile appears, and his dawning panic subsides.

"What do you say, Astronaut Bray?" he asks, raising his hand in a salute. "Did you bring your space boots?"

Jessie nods and puts both hands behind her back. When they reappear, they hold onto what can only be two pairs of invisible anti-gravity boots; a pair for him and a pair for her.

"When you've put them on, we'd better get going," Earl says. If he's annoyed by the persuasion session, he's hiding it well—which Nathan appreciates.

He's right, though. They do need to pull their fingers out.

Wearing his new space boots, Nathan takes the initiative and leads the way as they move toward the shoal of fish. He does so with large, bouncy steps and his arms stretched out to his sides as if trying to keep his balance under the gravity of this alien planet.

At first, Jessie stares at him with uncertain eyes, perhaps a bit embarrassed, but gradually she also starts to take part in the game. So does Meredith.

Earl obviously can't participate due to his injury. He has got his work cut out for him just trying to keep up with the others. Given the circumstances, however, he's doing quite well. He found an old plank that was half buried in the sand and uses it as a makeshift crutch. He's tired, of course, but he fights his exhaustion with a steady determination that Nathan admires.

As they approach the fish, Nathan realizes that he will need to muster something similar—a strong determination—if he's to find the courage to take the first step out among them.

The visual aspect is one thing, their dead eyes, and their mouths, continuously opening and closing, without a sound. That alone is scary enough, but in combination with the sporadic, squelching sounds of their scaly bodies clattering together, it's almost unbearable.

And the stench. Oh God, the stench.

"Astronaut Bray," he says, turning to Jessie. "I think we're going to need to activate our air filters."

With those words, he grabs the collar of Jessie's sweater and pulls it up so that it covers her mouth. Next, he does the same with his own shirt.

"Are we ready for the mission?"

"The floor is made of lava?"

"The floor is made of lava," Nathan repeats, raising his thumb.

In front of Jessie's mouth, the fabric of the sweater moves back and forth in time with her nervous breathing. Then it suddenly calms down and stops.

"Ready," she says, turning her thumb upward as well.

The first part of the way goes relatively smoothly. There are a lot of fish, but there are also plenty of patches of sandy bottom where they can land safely. Gradually, though, the balance between the two shifts, and as they approach the halfway mark, the distance between the safe landing zones is growing greater and greater.

"I think we'll need to double the force to get across here," Nathan says as they stop in front of a particularly difficult stretch.

"What do you mean?"

Instead of answering with words, Nathan reaches out his hand, letting it hang in the air until Jessie takes it.

"Two small steps and then one giant super jump. Are you with me, Astronaut Bray?"

"Uh-huh, yeah."

"They usually say *check*."

"Check."

"And your jetpack? Is it activated?"

"Yeah ... Um, check."

"Good. Then we'll take off in three, two, one, now!"

Jessie's burst of laughter only lasts a split second, and as soon as they touch down on the sand, it dies out again. But that one split second is enough for Nathan to hear it.

And it's a wonderful sound. Like a cold cloth on a forehead burning with fever.

It's almost a shame that it's followed by Earl's angry outburst, as the bottom of his improvised crutch slips in the sand, causing him to fall and end up on the ground with his right arm buried, all the way up to his elbow, in dead, slimy fish.

"OH, FUCKING SHIT!" he roars as he tries to get up but instead slides again so that half of his back also ends up down among the scaly animals. "THIS IS FUCKING GROSS!"

He says more than that, a lot more, but the words are muffled by a gurgling cough—and then completely choked as he suddenly bends down and vomits.

When it's over, Earl stays there for a while on his hands and knees, staring down at the pool of stomach acid and food remains he's just poured over the fish in front of him—and which is still connected to his chin by a thin thread of saliva.

"Do you need a hand to get up?" Nathan asks.

Earl shakes his head, making the spit thread

sway from side to side. Then he breaks it by letting out a hard, wheezing puff.

"You go ahead," he mutters. "I'll catch up."

Nathan opens his mouth and hesitates for a moment before closing it again without saying anything. Then he takes Jessie's hand and directs both her—and his own—focus onto the next jump on this grotesque obstacle course.

Thirteen jumps of varying difficulty later, the two self-proclaimed astronauts stand on the other side of the shoal of dying fish, waiting for the rest of their traveling party to cross the finish line. But before that happens, something else steals their attention.

A faint, shrill sobbing that, by Nathan's best estimate, comes from the back of a large boulder about two hundred yards from where they are standing. A massive, blue-gray rock whose glossy surface seems to reflect the light from the sky as if it's still wet ... which would make it the only one within miles.

At first, Nathan's brain tries to convince him that the sound could have come from a human being. A small child, younger than Jessie, who had somehow ended up out here in the middle of nowhere. Yet, the more he listens to it, the more he rejects that theory. Because beneath the human-like element in the sound lies something else. Something ... animal, guttural.

"What is that, Dad?"

"I don't know, sweetie. A seal or a sea lion, maybe."

"Is that how they sound?"

"Well, no, not exactly, but it could have been injured when the water disappeared."

"Like Captain Matthews and the other people who were on the ship with us?"

"Yeah," Nathan says, putting his arm around Jessie's shoulders. "Like them."

"So, they're dead now, right? Like Mom?"

For a moment, Jessie's question—and the innocent tone in which she asks it—makes Nathan's throat close up, and he has to concentrate not to let his emotions take over.

"Yeah, sweetie. Captain Matthews and the others are in heaven now. Just like Mom."

CHAPTER 7

Nathan was wrong on several accounts in his theory of the origin of the sound. It was a sea creature, but it was neither a seal nor a sea lion. His assumption that the animal was behind the large, round rock didn't hold true either. Because the animal isn't hiding behind the boulder. The animal *is* the boulder.

"Is it in a lot of pain?"

Before answering, Nathan lets his gaze drift along the body of the whale, hoping to spot some detail that would speak to the opposite.

He doesn't find anything. Its glossy, blue-gray skin shivers uneasily, its large, black eyes are locked in a glass-like stare, and its dorsal fin hangs limply as if the animal is on the verge of giving up the fight.

"It might not be hurting," says Earl, who is now

standing alongside Meredith a short distance behind them. "Physically, I mean. It's said that whales lose their sense of direction when stranded, and that's why they panic."

Jessie glances up at her father as if to confirm that Earl isn't just pulling her leg.

"Earl is right," Nathan confirms, nodding. "It's probably just confused and a little scared ... just like us."

"Can't we help it?"

"I wish we could, sweetie."

"Can I touch it?"

"It's too dangerous."

"But it doesn't look mad, Dad. It looks sad."

"It's not that I'm afraid it will hurt you on purpose," Nathan says, stroking his hand over the back of Jessie's head. "But it's very, very heavy. If we stand too close and it suddenly rolls over, it can get very dangerous."

Something gently touches Nathan's elbow. He turns around and is met by Meredith's wrinkled face. She stares at him with her brown eyes. Eyes that have seen generations grow up, witnessed their joy and sorrow—and right now, those eyes offer him a glimpse of her wisdom.

Perhaps an exception could be made this one time?

"You know what?" Nathan says, leaning down so

he can make eye contact with his daughter. "If we're very careful, I guess it would be okay to say hello."

Jessie's eyes light up and she starts to throw her arms up in the air, but Nathan stops her with a raised index finger.

"But we have to be very calm and careful, okay? You have to promise me that."

Jessie's face—at least everything except her eyes, which still glow with excitement—turns somber, and she nods.

"You have my word."

"I have your word?" Nathan repeats, smiling. "Oh, well, then say no more."

As they walk the rest of the way over to the stranded whale, Nathan takes the bag with the survival gear from the raft off his shoulder and rummages through it. Once he's located what he's looking for—the first-aid kit from before—he opens it and takes out the alcohol bottle.

"You keep that shit far away from me," Earl murmurs beside him. "I'm not falling for that one again."

For a moment, Nathan doesn't understand. Then his gaze slides down to the mechanic's bandage and he smiles.

"Don't worry. It's not for you. It's for our hands

afterward. A marine creature like this could be teeming with bacteria that are harmful to humans."

"I see. Better be on the safe side then."

That's what Earl says. Beneath the words, however, his tone of voice indicates that he finds such a concern rather pointless in their current predicament. He's probably right ... but what the hell else is Nathan supposed to do? After all, he can't just throw in the towel and give up. He has to keep hoping and insisting that things like that will matter again at some point, right?

And of course, there is still hope, he thinks to himself—but when he looks down at the bottle in his hand a second later, that thought is immediately challenged.

Because for a split second, it's not rubbing alcohol his brain sees splashing around behind the transparent plastic of the bottle.

It's water. Cold, refreshing water. He can almost taste it, feel it on his tongue and in his throat.

Fuck. How much time has passed since they got off the ship? A couple of hours? And he's already thirsty. If that's the case, the twelve water pouches in the emergency bag won't last very long.

"Um ... Nathan? Are you coming?"

"Huh? Oh, sorry," Nathan says, sending Earl a shaky smile. "I'm coming."

When they stop, now only five or six feet away from the giant sea creature, Nathan puts the emergency bag down on the sand and invites Jessie into his arms instead. She smiles, puts her arms around his neck, and lets him lift her up.

"It's really big," she whispers as Nathan warily approaches the awe-inspiring animal. He makes sure to position himself well in front of his pectoral fin— in case it should decide to give them a pat on the back with it.

"It sure is," Nathan replies. "But actually, there are whales that are way bigger."

"I know, Dad."

"Okay, okay, my bad. Do you also know what the biggest one is called?"

"The blue whale, right?"

Nathan smiles at her and nods. Then he takes another step closer. In doing so, he has brought them close enough for Jessie to reach out and touch the animal.

"It's hot."

"Whales are warm-blooded, just like humans," Nathan confirms, but Jessie doesn't seem to be listening. She's busy studying the structure of the whale's skin. Surprisingly, the animal doesn't seem to mind her touch. In fact, it appears to find it soothing. Its breathing gets calmer and its eyes blink slower.

"Bye, Mr. Whale," he hears Jessie whisper. "I'm sorry that you're stuck here, and I wish I could help you, but we have to go."

With those words, she pulls her hand back and turns to her father.

"I'm ready to go now."

Nathan doesn't say anything. He just nods, then turns his back on the whale and carries Jessie back to Earl and Meredith.

CHAPTER 8

Just how many miles they've covered as the evening sun begins to approach the line of the horizon to the west, Nathan doesn't have the faintest clue. Not enough. That's all he knows. Because they're still wading around on the muddled seabed, and as long as they're doing that, they haven't gotten far enough.

That they have made some sort of progress, however, is clear. On the one hand, they haven't been able to see where their footprints started for a while when they look back over their shoulders, and on the other hand, the muscles in his thighs feel as solid as concrete pillars. That's no wonder, though, as he hasn't just been carrying his own weight. With a traveling party consisting of an elderly woman, a seven-year-old girl, and a limping ship mechanic, Nathan has had to carry the emergency bag most of the time. And when he didn't have that on his shoulder, he often had Jessie in his arms instead. Because she's running flat too.

It's also high time to start looking for a place to camp for the night. He knows it, Earl knows it, and Meredith knows it. Yet it's as if all three of them have made a silent pact not to bring it up. As if they have some childish expectation that the sun might forget to set if they don't do anything to make it aware that the day is coming to an end.

But the sun couldn't care less about their wishful thinking. It follows its usual rhythm—and when it's time for its daily departure, it transforms the sky into an orange-red sea of flames.

And once that happens, there is no way around it.

"I'm thinking we camp under the leaning rock over there," Nathan says, pointing. "That'll give us some shelter if it gets windy during the night."

"I thought the same thing," Earl says, before looking over to Jessie and Meredith. "If you see any driftwood or anything else that will burn, then please bring it over there. There was a storm lighter in the emergency bag, but no fuel for a fire. And we are going to need a campfire, for food and for heat.

We don't know how cold it's going to be when it gets dark."

Jessie, who has been walking around in her own little world for some time with her eyes fixed on the sandy bottom, now suddenly lifts her head and looks up at the burning sky uncertainly. It's as if Earl's words, especially the last four—*when it gets dark*—have broken through a barrier in her mind and made her realize that they will have to spend the night out here.

And if Nathan is being honest with himself, something similar happened to him as well. He had thought about it, of course ... but he hadn't quite accepted it.

Without making a big deal of it, he gradually pulls to the right so that he comes closer to Jessie.

"It's going to be cool, huh? A bit like a camping trip."

"I don't want to sleep out here, Dad. It's scary."

As an almost sarcastic addition to those words, a series of small clicking sounds emerge from the ground slightly to the left of them. Two crabs fighting for the insides of a clam.

"I know, sweetie. But I think everything will look a bit brighter once we've gotten something to eat. Don't you think?"

"Maybe ... but I'm not really hungry. I'm thirsty."

Like a hand digging into his chest and tearing his heart out.

"Luckily, you won't have to wait too long," he replies. "We agreed to open the next water pouch with dinner. And I'm actually not that thirsty, so you can have a bit of my ration too. How about that?"

Jessie studies his face profoundly while he stubbornly holds the mask until she finally buys the lie and smiles.

"Thank you, Dad."

"You're welcome. Now, what do you say we try to find something Earl can use for the fire?"

"An excellent idea," says Earl, who apparently had half an ear on their conversation. "Get me some firewood and I'll fix you up the most delicious crab kebab you've ever tasted."

Nathan turns to Jessie, bringing his hands up to either side of his head and turning them as if snapping his invisible space helmet into place. Then he sends her an encouraging look.

"Understood, Astronaut Earl," she says, smiling as she also puts her helmet on. "We'll start the mission right away."

About three-quarters of an hour later, the mission is over, and all four of them sit in a semicircle around a campfire, staring impatiently at the six medium-sized crabs they have placed on a flat rock in the center.

Occasionally, Earl gets up on his good knee and moves a little closer to reposition the crabs. Every time, this causes the fire to send a cloud of embers soaring. Most die out almost immediately, but a few get caught by the wind and carried up along the rock wall behind them, conjuring up ominous shadows.

Technically, they wouldn't have had to eat crabs today, as there were some small food rations along with the water pouches in the emergency bag. However, they quickly agreed that it's better to eat what the sea has given them while they can ... because even though crabs can go for a while without water, they, too, won't last forever.

"I think they're just about ready," Earl says, tapping the crab shells. "Could you check to see if we remembered to pack the red wine in the bag, Meredith? If not, then just grab a water pouch."

This comment makes the adults in the group laugh—probably a little harder than it should have done, but in their defense, they are overtired.

"Sure, just a sec," Meredith says, after which she zips the bag open and pretends to rummage through it. "How about a Château Margaux. Will that do?"

"No, not that overrated mouthwash. We'll settle for water then."

"As you wish," Meredith says, handing a water pouch to Jessie. "You go right ahead, sweetheart."

Jessie glances at Nathan, receiving a nod of approval from him. She then takes a careful sip of the water, followed by another. Once done, she wipes her lips with the back of one hand while handing the water pouch to her dad with the other.

Nathan has never tasted the wine that Meredith referred to in her joke, so he has no idea if it's expensive or not, though he assumes that it is, based on her tone of voice. But what Nathan *does* know—without a shadow of a doubt—is that no wine in the world could hold a candle to the water hitting his palate right now.

A liquid fucking miracle. That's what it is, and it takes almost all his willpower to pull it away from his mouth again without emptying the pouch. How his seven-year-old daughter managed to do that is a mystery to him.

"Dinner is served," Earl says, making an inviting hand gesture in the direction of the crabs, which he has now placed on another stone next to the fire. "But be careful. They're a little hot."

The crabs aren't just *a little* hot. They're *red-hot*, and it feels like Nathan is on the verge of scorching off his fingerprints as he grabs one of the claws and breaks it into pieces so he can get to the meat inside.

But a burn or two is, his stomach tells him in a convincing growl, a fair price.

And right now, his stomach is in charge.

He hands the first piece of meat to Jessie, halfway expecting her to frown or at least hesitate a bit, given that seafood never was her favorite.

Jessie does neither. She grabs the meat, stuffs it in her mouth, and chews it with her eyes closed.

"I think the menu is approved," Nathan says, smiling at the chef.

But Earl doesn't seem to register him at all. He's sitting with a split crab claw in each hand, pulling white strands of flesh out of them with his teeth. Beside him, Meredith does the same—albeit with a slightly less animalistic approach. Nevertheless, their blissful facial expressions confirm Nathan's words quite clearly. The menu is definitely approved.

After the meal, they start arranging their sleeping spots. They don't have a lot to work with, but they do find four thin aluminum blankets in the emergency bag, one for each. It's far from optimal, but at least they don't have to worry about building a cover to protect themselves from moisture when the dew falls. In a world without water, that shouldn't be a problem.

That *has* to be the definition of cold comfort.

"Sleep well, sprout," Nathan whispers as he and

Jessie lie down between their two blankets. "I'm proud of you. You've been very brave today."

"Thank you, Dad, but ..."

"Yeah?"

"I ... I don't really feel brave anymore. And I don't think I can fall asleep out here."

"How about this; I'll be brave for you tonight. Then you can have a break. Would that be okay?"

Apparently, the answer is yes, because Jessie nods, crawls closer to him—and soon he can hear her breathing getting heavier.

For him, things move a bit slower. He lies there for a long time, staring blankly up at the bluish-black night sky above them, wondering if there is some mean-hearted god up there, finding this amusing.

And how much such a god must loathe him in order to force him to be brave for others and cling to a hope that is as fragile as a lone thread in a cobweb.

Again.

CHAPTER 9

"Do you understand what I'm saying to you, Mrs. Bray?"

No answer.

The doctor's gaze moves from Michelle's face to Nathan's, but there isn't much to be found there either. He's just as paralyzed as his wife. In fact, it feels as if the doctor's message has pushed Nathan's consciousness out of his body, leaving him to float freely in the air of the small office. Leaving him unable to do anything but stare in bewilderment as the doctor says words his brain can't or won't decode.

Words like scan results, lymph nodes, spread, malignant, chemotherapy, radiotherapy, and surgery.

Words like cancer.

"Mrs. Bray?" the doctor repeats, and although it's

Michelle the words are directed at, it's Nathan who wakes up with a twitch in his chair.

"I think we need a moment, if it's okay, Doctor?"

The doctor squints his eyes and stares at him hesitantly. Then he nods and gets up.

"Of course. Take a minute. I've also got some papers I need to hand in, so ..."

He says something more before walking out the door, but Nathan has stopped listening. His full attention is on Michelle, whose hand—ice-cold and trembling—he now takes in his own.

"We're gonna get through this, babe. I promise."

Michelle nods, but above the two wet lines on her cheeks, her eyes just keep staring blankly into the air.

"And you heard what he said, right? They have gotten really good at treating it with both chemo and ... and rays and everything."

"She's only two," Michelle whispers, still not looking at him.

"What was that?"

"Jessie. She's only two. If I die now, she won't remember me at all when she grows up."

"N-now, stop saying stuff like that, Michelle," Nathan says in a voice fragile as glass. "Of course, you're not gonna die. We ... it's going to be tough, sure, but we'll make it through. You'll get well again. I promise you."

Michelle pulls her hand away as if she's burned her

fingers and looks at him, stares at him, her eyes colder than he's ever seen them. It's as if they have somehow become devoid of life. As if she already—

No! he scolds himself inside his head. Don't you dare finish that thought!

"You and your promises," Michelle hisses out between her clenched teeth. "You don't know anything, Nathan. Anything!"

It would be a lie if Nathan claimed that those words didn't hit him like a fist in the diaphragm. But he understands where her anger is coming from, and he's willing to take both that punch and all the others that will inevitably follow in the time to come. Because that's what a partner does.

Therefore, he doesn't defend himself. He simply takes her hand in his once more and gives it a squeeze.

For a moment, Michelle looks down at his hands with the disapproval you'd expect to find in a schoolteacher who has just found a thumbtack on her chair. Then her tough facade crumbles, and she breaks down in tears.

Nathan puts an arm around her shoulder and leans closer to her. He says nothing because he doesn't have to. He just needs to be there.

Behind them, the door is opened with a faint creak. It's Dr. Pearson, who has returned. He sends Nathan an inquiring look, and when the answer is a small nod, he pushes the door shut behind him and walks over to his office chair.

"I realize that it can be very overwhelming to get a message like this," he says. "But as I said earlier, there's been a lot of progress in cancer research over the past years."

He hesitates for a moment as he leans in over the table and rubs his hands against each other. Then he spreads them to the sides and sits back in his chair.

"Now, don't get me wrong," he says. "I obviously can't give any guarantees."

"N-no, um, obviously."

"But if we start treatment asap, there's a fair chance we can prevent the cancer from spreading further ... or at least prolong her life considerably."

Out of the corner of his eye, Nathan sees his wife put her hands up in front of her mouth as she lets out a gasp. His own hands remain on the armrests of the chair, but their knuckles turn white as chalk.

"And, um ... what now?" he manages to stutter. "I mean, what's next?"

"The next step is that we make a plan for the treatment. This also includes a detailed outline of the entire process, so you know exactly what's going to happen and when it's going to happen."

"Okay. That's ... that's nice."

"Yes, it's easier for the patients that way," the doctor

says, nodding in a slow, pensive manner that for some reason really pisses Nathan off. Maybe it's because Dr. Pearson sounds more like a robot reading from a textbook than an actual human being right now. "Furthermore, you will be put in touch with a specialist who will accompany you throughout the process, and we also have psychologists and social workers who can help you with all the practical and emotional challenges."

"Well, that sounds good, doesn't it, babe?" *Nathan says, caressing Michelle's shoulder.*

She doesn't answer him.

"But even though we will do what we can to make it easier, you should of course expect that your life will be turned upside down in the coming months," *the doctor continues.* "For instance, you'll need to do the heavy lifting at home, Nathan."

"Yeah, of course. That's no problem."

"As I said, it's perfectly normal to feel overwhelmed and scared. But remember that you have each other. And you have your family and friends. You should never be afraid to ask for help or talk about your feelings. That's important."

The doctor pauses as he rubs his thumb over a large, dark brown knot in the wood under the glossy surface of the desk.

"Do you have any questions?" *he then says.*

Nathan and Michelle exchange a glance, and again

the thought crosses Nathan's mind that her eyes look as if all signs of life have already seeped out of them.

"When does treatment begin?" he asks.

The doctor nods with his lower lip shot forward as if to say, 'excellent question.'

"At least within the next two weeks," the doctor states, with an uneasy grin. "It's a legal requirement. However, my guess would be that Michelle will get a call as early as the beginning of next week."

"So, you'll contact us?"

"Yes, of course. Any other questions?"

"No, I think we just need to get home now. Give it a chance to sink in, you know?"

The doctor nods. Then he reaches out his hand.

Nathan takes it, shakes it, and says thank you.

Michelle doesn't.

DAY 2

CHAPTER 10

When Nathan opens his eyes the next morning, none of the others have woken up. Jessie is still lying with her face pressed against his chest, breathing in long, heavy sighs, while Earl and Meredith lie, each under their own blanket, on the other side of yesterday's fire, now just a depressing pile of gray ash.

The sky is also gray and depressing. Dark clouds everywhere and no sign of the sun or wind to chase them away.

Carefully, as to not wake her up, he lifts Jessie's head slightly so he can pull his arm free, after which he slithers out of the blanket by rolling sideways in a gentle, controlled motion.

Once up in a sitting position, he pauses, partly because his spine feels like it's been twisted a few times around itself, and partly because he spots the shell of a conch half-buried in the sand in front of his foot.

He picks it up, studies it—and is hit by a deep sense of discouragement when a thought strikes him. It comes in the form of a phrase that most parents at one time or another have said to their child, and that he himself has also said to Jessie.

If you hold it up to your ear, you can hear the song of the sea in it.

The song of the sea, waves rolling in on the shore. One of the world's most soothing sounds ... and now a thing of the past.

He sighs and throws the conch back into the sand. Then he gets up and starts gathering wood for the fire so they can have a warm breakfast when the others get up.

His first impulse is to gather some fish and fry them, but after thinking it through, he realizes that it's probably best to stick to the shellfish. Sure, they have a Swiss Army knife in the emergency bag that he could use for gutting the fish, but if he intends to wash his hands clean afterward, the only solution is to open a water pouch, and that's off the table.

So, looks like it's crab again this morning.

While Nathan is building a pyramid of small

pieces of wood and strips of dried seaweed, Earl wakes up with a jolt. He looks at Nathan, then at the dry, gray landscape, and finally down at the bandage on his leg.

"Good morning," Nathan says.

Earl raises one eyebrow and squints at him as if to say: *What's good about it?*

"Uh-huh, good morning. Sorry that I'm not thrilled to see you. I might have hoped it was all just a bad dream."

"That makes two of us. How's the leg?"

"Not too good," Earl says, contorting his face as he touches the dressing. "It feels warm. I'm starting to worry that it might be infected."

Nathan nods, biting his lower lip—which prompts Earl to quickly raise his hands and add:

"But don't worry, I can still walk if that's what you're thinking about."

"No, no, it wasn't."

That is an outright lie. That was exactly what went through Nathan's head. Because he has his daughter to think about, and he's eerily aware that their chances of surviving long enough to make it to the islands are close to nonexistent. And if, on top of that, Earl can't even walk ...

It's an unpleasant thought, but it's nothing compared to the one that now briefly swims by in his subconscious, like a scaly crocodile beneath a muddy water surface.

The president himself could pick you up in Air Force One right here and now, and it still wouldn't make a difference. No water equals no life. As a marine biologist, you should know that. It's page one of the textbook.

"How's the little astronaut doing?" Earl asks, nodding toward Jessie.

"Pretty good, all things considered. She woke up once last night feeling a little scared, but other than that, she's slept like a log."

"That's a tough gal you've got there. Did you, um ... I mean, are you alone with her?"

"Yeah, I raised her myself. We lost her mother when Jessie was four. Cancer. Since then, it's just been me and her."

"Fucking shitty disease."

"Oh, yeah," Nathan says bitterly, after which he checks the fire and starts placing their breakfast on the round stone in the middle. "We can start waking up the others, I think."

"I'm awake," Jessie mumbles, but it seems to be only partly true. Her voice is slurred, her eyes are still closed, and instead of sitting up, she curls up in a fetal position under the blanket.

Meredith, on the other hand, sits up immediately when Earl gently places a hand on her shoulder and asks if she's awake. And like him, she starts the new day by looking around perplexed, only to let out a heavy sigh once the pieces fall into place.

"Yeah, sorry," Nathan says. "We're still here."

Meredith makes a labored swallowing motion and nods. She looks like she's struggling to hold back tears.

Nathan opens his mouth to say a few words of encouragement to her, but when none comes to him, he closes it again and turns to Earl instead.

"Would you mind taking the chef's position for a sec?"

Earl nods and scooches closer to the fire. In the meantime, Nathan walks over to Jessie and strokes her hair.

"Are you coming, sweetie? Breakfast is just about ready."

"I don't want crabs again," Jessie mutters, pulling the blanket up in front of her face. "I want to go home, and I want cornflakes."

"But what about the mission? We haven't found out if there are sea turtles on Oceania yet."

"Oceanus," Jessie corrects.

"Oh yeah, sorry. My bad. But won't you please get up? I don't know if I can handle the mission alone."

He leans down to her, lowering his voice to a whisper, and adds:

"Especially if I have to keep an eye on Earl and Meredith as well. They're like two unruly toddlers, those two."

"Hey, I heard that," says Meredith, who—to Nathan's relief—seems to have regained control of her emotions.

"What do you say, Astronaut Bray? Don't you want to help me find a sea turtle? Wasn't that the whole reason you went on the trip in the first place?"

Slowly, the silvery aluminum blanket slides downward, revealing Jessie's beautiful, freckled face, whose expression gradually moves from one of hesitant skepticism to one of excitement and anticipation.

And there, at that very moment, it's clear to Nathan. Whatever happens, his daughter is gonna get to see a sea turtle in the wild. No matter the cost.

CHAPTER 11

When the hour hand on his wristwatch jumps to the number three half a day later, Nathan has just completed a depressing calculation in his head.

If a person is in good health, has energy, and a full stomach, he or she will be able to walk approximately fifteen miles in one day on level terrain. He believes he has read that somewhere. And on average, a human being will only be able to survive for three to ten days without water. He believes he has read that too.

His memory could be betraying him, of course. The problem is that he can add a margin of error of about fifty percent on both factors, and it still leads to the same result: They're screwed.

Why? They were about sixty miles from shore

when the ship went down. The terrain is anything but level. They covered a maximum of three miles yesterday. They have an injured man, a child, and an old lady in the group.

Not to mention that they, despite fairly strict rationing, have already emptied four of the twelve water pouches that were in the emergency bag.

Big-time screwed.

Aware that he has to get off that train of thought if it isn't to drive him mad, Nathan slows his pace, so he ends up walking next to Meredith, who is studying a cluster of dried red algae.

"Why were you even on that ship? I have been meaning to ask you. Because you weren't part of the crew, were you?"

"No, I wasn't. I ... well, I guess you could say I was on vacation."

"On a cargo ship?"

Meredith shrugs and smiles.

"It was my friend who arranged it. She knows ... no, she knew Captain Matthews, and she knew I'd like to experience life on board a ship."

She pauses, staring thoughtfully into the air. Then she shakes her head.

"Actually, it was a very old dream. My old man was a sailor, you see, and he passed away when I was quite young. I think that's why I've always been attracted to the idea of sailing. I guess I figured that it would bring me closer to him. But sailing on a *real* ship, you know? Not one of those holiday cruisers."

"And why only now?" Nathan asks. "If it was such an old dream, I mean."

"Well, good question. The course of life is probably the short answer. In my youth, I never got around to it, and when I found me a husband who suffered from both fear of flying and fear of water, well ... I kind of shelved the idea. But after I lost George last year, it started popping up in the back of my mind again. Then one day I happened to mention it to my friend. And yeah, the rest is history, as they say."

She squints her eyes as if rewinding her story in her head to check that everything was correct. Then she nods and lets her gaze wander over the barren and desolate plain they are on right now. A plain strewn with dead sea creatures and parched plants.

"Had I known that I would end up here, that dream might have stayed on the shelf. But oh well, I've lived long enough to know that it's a waste of time to worry about things that you don't have the power to change anyway."

This last sentence leaves Nathan speechless. For it's one thing to throw out an expression like that. They do, after all, come in countless variations. But to deliver it in such a calm and serene voice when caught in the middle of this hell ... that's no small thing.

And he finds that he buys it. He truly believes that the little, gray-haired lady walking beside him—slightly hunched and with her coat tied around her waist because the temperature has risen during the day—actually means every word. And accepts them.

Part of him wishes he could do the same. Another part of him—a larger part—prays that he will never get to that point.

Instinctively, his gaze slides over to Jessie. She is walking alongside Earl a little farther behind. It looks like she's showing him something. Maybe a pretty stone or a seashell.

"What's the situation in the rearguard? Can you keep up?"

"I wouldn't complain about a break and a sip of water," Earl replies. "The yellow fireball up there is brutal today."

Nathan raises his hand to his forehead to shield his eyes as he squints up at the sun. It has come out now, yes, and the temperature *is* higher than it was this morning. Still, calling the sun *brutal* today is a stretch. Moreover, Nathan strongly suspects that it's not the sun that bears the primary responsibility for the ship mechanic sweating like a horse. A more likely explanation is that the wound under the bandage on his lower leg has become inflamed and that his body, in an attempt to fight the infection, has entered into a state of fever.

"We can take a rest once we get over the hill, so we don't have to start out with crossing that right after," Nathan says, pointing. "Does that sound fair?"

Earl frowns but nevertheless answers with a raised thumb.

In the end, they don't make it all the way across the rocky hill before they stop. Because upon reaching the top, they get a view of the landscape on the other side. The next stretch of their journey. And the next obstacle.

"Someone up there really hates us," Earl groans.

"You can say that again," Nathan replies, even though the marine biologist in him is tempted to correct a detail of Earl's statement. Because *someone up there* might have put them here ... but it's not *someone up there* who is responsible for the mess at the foot of the hill. That's on humans.

"What *is* that?" he hears Jessie ask.

"Chemical waste," he replies bitterly. "Someone has used the seabed as a landfill and dumped chemical waste out here."

Only now, saying it out loud, does he become aware of the stench. How intrusive and rancid it is.

Somehow his brain must have shut off his sense of smell. Probably to spare him the scent of dead fish that have surrounded them for the last twenty-four hours.

They're lying everywhere, barrels and metal containers of different sizes, some in large piles, others scattered aimlessly. A large proportion of them has rusted so much after spending years at the bottom of the ocean that it looks as if they have merged with the reddish sand. For the same reason, many of them are leaky and have spilled tons of oil and other toxic chemicals. These hazardous liquids now pool in crevices and depressions in the lifeless landscape, forming small, black-green lakes and canals.

Over the entire area hangs a faint, flickering mist. Like the one you would find hovering above an asphalt road on a particularly hot summer day. Minus the blue-green glow that the fog over the barrels has, of course.

Nathan turns around to tell his young space-traveling colleague that it's time to reactivate the air filters of their helmets, but Jessie is one step ahead of him. She has pulled her blouse up so that it covers her mouth. He winks approvingly at her, then turns to Earl.

"I'm afraid we'll have to settle for a quick sip of

water and save the break until we're past this."

"Never mind," Earl says. "I'm not exactly keen on sitting here, chatting away while our lungs are filled with that stuff, anyway."

Nathan gives him a nod and a smile, then pulls out a water pouch from the bag and hands it to him.

While Earl drinks and subsequently passes the water on to Jessie and Meredith, Nathan once again lets his gaze wander across the landscape ahead.

"The quickest route would be to go straight through," he says. "But to be on the safe side, I think we'd better stay on the edge of the, um ..."

For a moment, he can't find the right word. His brain suggests *valley*, but he finds that far too positive.

"The crater," Meredith says, and he nods. That has exactly the right ring to it. Like something from a horror story.

"Keeping to the edges sounds fine," Earl says. "I won't protest to that."

"Me neither," Meredith adds, after which she takes a few sips from the water pouch and hands it back to Nathan.

"Good," he says once he has taken his share of the precious liquid and packed the now almost empty water pouch back into the emergency bag. "Then let's get it over with."

CHAPTER 12

A moment's inattentiveness. As most parents of young children know, sometimes that's all it takes for a situation to go completely off track, letting all hell break loose.

As they walk along the outer edge of the chemical-filled depression in the landscape, which Meredith named the *crater*, Nathan gets to feel that truth in full.

Because for a few seconds, his conversation with Earl takes his focus, so he doesn't register that Jessie lets go of his hand. And by the time he realizes it, she's already made her way out there. Out onto the dark brown, scab-like ground that marks the rim of the crater.

Now she stands there, both feet planted on the cracked surface, while small bubbles full of toxic gases emerge in the sticky mud that can be spotted beneath the crevices.

"Jessie! What are you doing? Get away from there."

"It's okay, Dad," she says, taking another step without even looking back in his direction, after which she bends down and picks up some object. "It's just that there's something inside of it, and I want to see what it is."

"Inside of it? What are you—"

A faint creaking, resembling the sound of a hinge that needs grease, is followed by three sharp snaps, like a stick breaking after being flicked against something hard.

And then the ground starts to give way. New cracks emerge, and before Jessie has time to realize what is happening, one of her feet has sunk into the slimy mud.

"Dad, help!" she cries as the mud swallows more and more of her leg as if a living being—a giant, slimy mutant snail born of the toxic chemicals—is trying to devour it.

Now, almost like an eerie extension of this image, a large bubble bursts behind Jessie with exactly the sound that one would imagine such a creature making if it burped.

"Stay where you are!" Nathan shouts as he runs to the rim of the crater, hesitates, and then starts setting his foot down in various places, hoping to find a spot where the fragile crust can support his weight. "Don't move. It'll only make you sink quicker."

Jessie's face contracts in a mixture of panic and dread, but at least she listens to him and stays in place.

No, that's a lie. She doesn't move, but she doesn't stay in place either, because now the crust also breaks under her other leg ... which means she sinks into the poisonous mud twice as fast.

"Hold on, Jessie! I'm coming out to you!"

Somewhere on the fringes of his consciousness, Nathan knows full well that it's a crazy solution that will only worsen the situation. But at this moment, rational thoughts aren't what drives him. Instinct is. The urge to protect his daughter at all costs. So, he takes a deep breath, backs some distance away from the edge of the crater, locks his gaze on Jessie ... and starts running.

He's inches from taking off and sealing his own destiny when Earl's hand grabs the back of his shirt and pulls him backward.

"Look at it!" Earl orders, pointing at the mud.

"That shit is like fucking quicksand. If you jump out there, you'll just sink in too."

Nathan glances out there and feels a mixture of dismay and guilt build up inside of him, realizing that the ship mechanic is right.

"Here," Earl says, dropping the worn plank he's been using as a crutch onto the cracked crust to form a bridge out to Jessie. "Step on that instead so the weight is distributed."

Nathan nods, then gently places a foot on the plank, which—amazingly—seems pretty stable. He double-checks one more time by pressing his foot downward, and seeing that the plank stays in place, he takes two quick steps forward, bringing him out in the middle, where he slides down to one knee in a slow, controlled motion.

"Take my hand."

Jessie shifts her gaze to his hand but doesn't take it. In fact, she looks like she's staring right through it.

"Jessie, sweetie? I know you're scared, but you have to help me a little here, okay? Otherwise, I can't get you up."

This time, he seems to get through to her. In any case, she starts moving her hand toward his. But only the one. The other she uses to keep the object she picked up before pressed against her chest. It's an empty wine bottle, he can see now.

"I need both your hands, sweetie. You can throw the bottle to Earl if you want."

"I'll catch it," Earl says immediately.

Jessie hesitates for a moment, looking down at the bottle. Then she lifts it up and throws it to Earl.

"Good," Nathan says. "Now give me your hands."

Jessie obeys, and as soon as he has a firm grip on her hands, he starts pulling her toward the plank. At first, it feels like an almost impossible task, but gradually the mud lets go and releases her from its grip.

Once Jessie is close enough to the edge for Meredith and Earl to reach her, they take over and help her safely ashore. Afterward, they do the same for her father.

"What were you thinking?" Nathan asks once his heart rate has lowered enough for him to communicate without either scolding or breaking down.

"I'm sorry, Dad," Jessie sniffles. "I just wanted to see what was on the paper."

"What paper?"

The answer comes immediately. Not from Jessie, but from the bottle that Earl now hands him. And as Nathan takes a closer look at it, everything suddenly makes a lot more sense.

The wine bottle isn't empty like he thought. There is a rolled-up piece of paper inside.

A message in a bottle. In this dead, barren desert,

which just twenty-four hours ago was an ocean full of life, his seven-year-old daughter has found a freaking message in a bottle.

You can hardly blame her for bending the rules a little to retrieve it.

CHAPTER 13

Ahoy!

My name is Tommy Timberleg, and I'm a dangerous pirate! No, don't worry, it's not true, haha! I'm just a nine-year-old boy from Pennsylvania.

In my class, we're learning about pirates, and then we all had to send a message in a bottle.

A little about me: I like G.I. Joe and Trans-formers, and I live in East Alin with my mom and my dad and my little brother. If you find my bottle, please send me a letter and let me know. My address is ...

Tommy Morgan
3 Maple Lane
East Alin, PA 17213-4272
United States

"He sounds nice. Do you think we can write to him when we get home?"

Nathan looks down at the letter in Jessie's hands and then up at her freckled face. She looks so tiny sitting there, wrapped in her aluminum blanket next to Meredith, who is holding the girl's pants and shoes in her lap, trying to clean them using sand. So tiny and so innocent. Like a silvery version of Little Red Riding Hood.

"Yeah, maybe," he limits his answer to. He could have elaborated with the analysis he has done in his head and explained how it was hardly worth it, since little Tommy, who loves G.I. Joe and Transformers, presumably is in his late forties by now and may well have changed his address a few times since the eighties. Not to mention the whole *when we get home* issue.

But Jessie is seven years old, trapped on a parched seabed with three adults, and she has just found someone she can identify with and devote some of her focus to.

So, in Nathan's eyes, a *yeah, maybe* seems like a reasonable compromise.

"You really think that's gonna work?" he asks, nodding down at the pants that Meredith is scrubbing with a handful of sand.

"A little elbow grease can work wonders," Meredith replies, holding up one leg of the pants so he can see. Astonishingly, she has actually managed to get most of the mud off, leaving only a dark stain on the fabric. "If we put a bag or piece of the aluminum coating from one of the blankets under her pants and socks, I think it'll be okay."

"As long as it doesn't touch her skin, it should work," Earl adds. He's sitting behind Meredith, working on his own sand-cleaning project. And like her, he has gotten a fairly impressive result. His crutch—the plank they used to get Jessie out of the mud—is back to its normal self.

Half an hour later, Nathan is on his knees in front of Jessie, checking that the improvised barriers between her skin and the dark gray chemical stains on her pants are properly placed.

It seems okay. The shoes included. Some of the gear in the emergency bag was wrapped in small plastic bags, and they wrapped two of them around her feet.

"Is it approved?" Meredith asks, and Nathan replies with a raised thumb.

"It's perfect, Meredith. Thank you so much."

Meredith makes a *don't mention it* gesture with her hand, then turns around and walks over to Earl, who is sitting on a rock, examining his bandage. Meanwhile, Nathan turns back to Jessie.

"Did you know they use that kind of aluminum for making real spacesuits?" he asks—and when Jessie shakes her head, he adds, "It's to protect them from the cold out in space, I think. So, in a way, you've got a *real* space suit now. That's pretty cool, huh?"

Jessie smiles and nods ... but it's not the most convincing smile he's seen from her.

"It *is* cool," she says. "But I thought that maybe we could be something other than astronauts today."

"I see. What did you have in mind?"

Jessie shrugs and lets her gaze wander upward, pretending to need time to think about the answer—which Nathan knows full well she doesn't.

"Um, I don't know ... pirates, maybe?"

"Like the boy in the letter," Nathan says, nodding. "You know what, sweetie? That sounds like a great idea."

Jessie smiles again, this time convincingly, and Nathan takes her hand and pulls her to her feet. Next, with one leg stiff as if it were made of wood, he walks toward Earl and Meredith.

"Ahoy, you landlubbers! If you're done slacking

off, Captain Jolly Jessie and myself suggest we move on."

Earl gazes at him with one eyebrow raised, as if to say: *Where did you find those pills?* Meredith, on the other hand, catches on immediately.

"Of course," she says, winking at Jessie. "No need to ready the plank for us. We'll be right there."

Satisfied with the answer—and with her new role as a pirate captain—Jessie nods to Meredith before spinning around on her heel and gesturing them to join her in the continued march southwest.

A few seconds later, her crew obediently follows.

CHAPTER 14

The campsite for their second night in this unforgiving desert is almost identical to that of the previous night. The firepit has the same structure, a small excavation in the sand and a flat stone in the middle, and they have once again built it close to a rock to have shelter from the wind. The food is also similar—although it doesn't taste nearly as good. It turns out that grilled crab meat loses some of its magic when eating it for the fourth time within twenty-four hours.

Even the way they're sitting around the firepit while eating is almost the same; Meredith and Jessie sit with their blankets wrapped around them, Nathan sits cross-legged, and Earl half sits, half lies with most of his weight placed on his good leg to spare the other.

Despite all these common traits with the night before, though, one thing is significantly different.

The mood. It's darker and more dense. It's as if the metaphorical light of hope disappeared along with the light of the sun as it crept down behind the horizon. As if the bitter reality has reached their collective consciousness at exactly the same time.

Three water pouches left.

Tomorrow they *will* run out of water.

After the meal, they remain seated around the fire for a good while, doing nothing but staring blankly into the air, listening to the soft crackle of the burning wood.

No one says anything because no one has anything to say. Even Jessie, who doesn't fully grasp the magnitude of it all, seems to have run out of words. She sits with one shoulder leaning against Nathan's arm, fiddling with the hem of his sleeve. It's a habit she's had since she was very little, and usually, it means she's getting tired.

So is Nathan. In body and in soul alike. So tired that he can't even muster the energy to try to cheer Jessie up.

But what would you even say to her, anyway? he

thinks bitterly. *That everything will look brighter tomorrow? That it always helps to sleep on it?*

In the end, it is Earl who breaks the silence as he gets up to answer nature's call but accidentally puts too much weight on his bad leg.

What the mechanic's exact words are, Nathan can't quite decipher, as they're intertwined with frustrated groans and growls. Nevertheless, there is no doubt that it belongs in the category of profanities.

"Have you had the bandage off today?" he asks.

"Not entirely," Earl says. "I've loosened the bandage to glimpse at it a couple of times. That's all."

"And how does it look?"

Earl makes a strained grimace and shrugs.

"Let's just say I wouldn't turn down a bottle of penicillin." He hesitates, then lets out a snort and adds, "Hell, there aren't many things I wouldn't do for a handful of good old-fashioned painkillers right now, to be honest."

"Yes, that's been bothering me too, why there weren't any pills in the first-aid kit," Meredith interjects—prompting Earl to let out another burst of air through his nostrils.

"Oh, I can solve that mystery for you," he says, shaking his head resignedly. "Lenny Phelps."

"Lenny Phelps?" Nathan repeats. "As in the kitchen help?"

"Yup. That little pale-skinned weekend junkie made a habit of emptying all of the ship's medicine cabinets, taking everything that was to be found in them. And it wouldn't surprise me in the least if he also made a stop or two by the life rafts on one of his pilfering trips. If that little shit was here right now, I tell you ..."

He finishes his sentence by holding out his hands and shaking them as if they were closing around an invisible neck.

"But he's not here," Meredith mutters, sighing. "We all know where Lenny is now."

Earl lowers his hands and stares at her with a strangely hesitant look. Then he shrugs, grabs his crutch, and makes another attempt to get up. This time he succeeds, and he walks around behind the cliff to relieve himself.

In the meantime, Nathan gets up from his seat by the fire and starts preparing their sleeping spots on the sand. His tired muscles protest wildly as he spreads one of the blankets on the ground, but he ignores their complaints and continues.

As soon as their sad excuse for a mattress is ready, Jessie carries her blanket over and settles under it. The full process is carried out with slow, drowsy movements, almost to the point where you would think she was sleepwalking.

But Jessie doesn't sleep. Not then, nor ten minutes later when Nathan lays down next to her. Her breathing is heavy, but her eyes are still open. They stare up at the stars, which sparkle like precious gems sprinkled over a blue-black velvet mat.

"You having trouble falling asleep?" he whispers, brushing a loose tuft of hair away from her face.

Jessie shrugs and moves closer to him. Her gaze isn't moving anywhere, though. It stays fixated on the stars. On this light from distant galaxies that still hits their eyes, even though the suns from which it comes may have burned out and ceased existing long ago.

Perhaps these are the kind of thoughts that tumble around in there behind Jessie's innocent eyes.

"Dad?"

"Yes, sweetie?"

"Who is G.I. Joe?"

For a moment, Nathan comes dangerously close to bursting into laughter, but he manages to suppress the reflex.

"It's not so much a *who* as it is a *what*," he says. "It's a toy that a lot of boys liked to play with in the past. They're a kind of action figure."

"Can you still buy them?"

"I actually don't know. Maybe."

"If you can, I'd like to send one along if we write a letter to Tommy when we get home."

"That's a lovely idea," Nathan replies, turning his face away under the pretext of glancing at the fire. "But now we'd better go to sleep, okay? We have a long day tomorrow."

"Okay. Good night, Dad."

"Good night, sweetie."

With those words, Nathan closes his eyes and replaces the velvet mat of the night sky with another darkness. Soon after, he also replaces this day's agonizing nightmare with another. One that—as it usually does—takes him back to another time in his life.

CHAPTER 15

As she lies there, dressed in a blue hospital gown, Michelle Bray is but a shadow of herself. Her face is ashen gray, her hair is gone from the chemo treatment, and she has a piece of tape over the back of her left hand from when they took a blood test about an hour ago.

She is in pain all the time. Even now, when she's dozing off, he can see it on her. Tiny twitches in her lips and cheeks, as if every five seconds the device she's hooked up to gives her an electric shock instead of medication.

Nathan is also in pain. Not in the same way as Michelle, of course. His pain isn't visible to the naked eye the way hers is. In fact, he does everything he can to keep it hidden.

But it's always there. Like a parasite inside him that feeds itself by draining his life force.

Over in the bed, Michelle jerks uneasily, and he instinctively puts his hand on top of hers, caressing it. It feels fragile and skeletal. As if the bones beneath her skin could shatter if he applied even the slightest pressure.

She opens her eyes and stares at him with an unstable, flickering gaze.

"Why are you still here?"

"I promised the minister that I would be," Nathan says, holding up his hand as he moves the finger on which his wedding ring resides.

"Don't. You know what I mean. Why aren't you at home with Jessie?"

"My parents offered to take her to the zoo, and I said yes. Thought it might be good for her to get out of the house a bit."

Michelle moves her hand down and feels her way along the metal frame of the bed until her fingers find the remote control to raise and lower the mattress. It's a small movement, and the whole process only takes a few seconds. Still, it's enough to make her moan and grimace.

With a drowsy, electric hum, the motor lifts the top half of the mattress upward, bringing Michelle up to eye level with Nathan.

"It's important that she doesn't feel alone," she says. Not angrily, but with a hint of discontent in her voice. "It's bad enough that I can't take care of her. I don't want her to blame me for stealing you too."

"Jessie isn't alone. She's with her grandma and grandpa. And she doesn't blame you for anything. That's a crazy thing to say."

"Is it?"

"She's three years old, Michelle."

"I know, but if I don't survive this, I don't want it to be the only thing she remembers about me, that I was the reason why her dad was never home."

"If you don't survive? Tell me, where the hell is this coming from? You can't just throw in the towel like that and give up. I mean, we have to keep hoping, right? Otherwise—"

He doesn't get any further before Michelle slams both her hands into the duvet.

"WHAT WE HAVE TO DO, NATHAN, IS WAKE UP AND START FACING REALITY! I'M SICK, AND NO MATTER HOW NAUSEATINGLY OPTIMISTIC YOU INSIST ON BEING, IT DOESN'T CHANGE THE FACT THAT THIS SHIT IS PROBABLY GOING TO KILL ME!"

She's worn out, she's in pain, and it's not the first time she's tried to taunt him like that. But it's the closest she's been to succeeding—and that scares him.

The worst part is that he has a feeling that she, at least in part, is doing it for his sake. That deep down, she hopes he will storm out of the room in anger, slam the door behind him, and never come back. Because if he does that, if he says fuck this shit and forgets all about her, he'll be free. Let out of the cage that she believes her illness has locked him and Jessie in.

But he's not going anywhere, and he lets her know that now—not with words, but by staying silently in the chair next to her bed until the anger in her gaze slowly subsides, letting grief take its place and thus reveal that it was the true villain all along.

"Oh God, Nathan," she sobs, gently touching his hand. "I don't know what got into me."

"Chemo, pain, and stress," Nathan says, closing his fingers around hers. "You're just exhausted, that's all. Tomorrow you'll feel better, and then everything will look much brighter. Then you'll be the nauseating optimist. Just wait and see."

That's what Nathan says to her.

He hopes, with all his heart, that it holds true.

DAY 3

CHAPTER 16

As it creeps downward in small jerks on the inside of the transparent plastic that slowly crumbles around it, Nathan's gaze follows along. He sees it getting pulled out of the water pouch to then disappear into his daughter's mouth.

It's 1:46 p.m., and the last drop—their *very last* drop of water—is now officially gone. From this moment on, the hourglass can no longer be flipped upside down. Once the remaining grains of sand have made their way to its bottom, it's over.

That thought causes an icy chill to run through Nathan's spine, and he forces himself to push it aside.

"At least we'll have shade on the next stretch," he hears Meredith say, and for a split second, it almost feels like she's been listening in on his thoughts, trying to help him find something positive to latch onto.

And for what it's worth, she's right. They will be shaded from the relentless midday sun for a while, as they are entering a large area full of rocks that rise like obelisks from the barren sand, sharp and ruthless.

To get through this rough maze of rocks, they will need to squeeze through narrow crevices and walk under large, jammed boulders. All while shrouded in the semi-darkness of the shadows, which makes it seem as if the large rocks have swallowed up the light and left them in a world of only gray shades.

Something about this place gives him the creeps —and a brief glance down at Jessie is sufficient to tell him she feels the same way.

This might be the right time to give her the gift he made for her this morning while the others were still sleeping.

"I almost forgot, Captain," he says, sliding his hand into his pants pocket. "I've got something for you."

Jessie stares at him with a mixture of surprise and suspicion in her eyes, but when she sees what it is he has hidden in his pocket, both vanish instantly. They are replaced by delight.

"You can't really call yourself a true pirate captain without one, can you?" Nathan says as he hands her the gift.

Jessie accepts it, ties it around her head, and adjusts it until the flap sits perfectly in front of one eye.

"Thank you, Dad!"

"You're welcome, sweetie. I didn't have any thread, so I had to cut it all in one piece ... and yeah, I know they're usually black, but I only had the silvery fabric from the blanket."

"It's perfect, Dad," she says, giving him a hug before turning toward the other two and posing for them with her back straight and a hand on one hip as if she were an actual pirate captain looking out over the ocean from the bow of her ship.

"It's beautiful," Meredith says.

"Classic yet modern," Earl adds, drawing his lips up into what undoubtedly should have been a smile but ends up being more of a strained grimace.

A grimace that tells Nathan that the mechanic probably lied this morning when asked how his leg was doing today.

Half an hour later that thought is confirmed when Earl slowly starts to fall behind and then stops completely, groaning and panting, as he leans against one of the large boulders.

"Let me see that leg," Nathan says, his tone of voice stressing that it isn't a polite request but a direct order.

Earl scowls and stares at him with narrowed eyes as he breathes in and out of his nostrils like a stressed bull. Then he closes his eyes and gives in with a resigned nod.

"You can sit here," Meredith says, patting a small ledge at the bottom of a rock.

Earl does as he's told and staggers over there, and when he has taken a seat, Nathan squats down in front of him and starts to loosen the bandage very gently.

"Christ, Earl," he blurts out, having pulled off enough to reveal what's behind the bandage.

The wound is hideous. A grotesque mixture of pus, blood, and discolored tissue that flow together, forming a mosaic of decay. The skin around the oozing wound is red and swollen, brimming with inflammation. The smell that hangs around his calf muscle is the bitter, suffocating stench of rot. The scent of death.

"Why didn't you tell us it was this bad?" Nathan groans, even though part of him suspects he knows the answer.

"What difference would it make?" Earl says. "In case you haven't noticed, we don't have oceans of time, no pun intended. Besides, I haven't seen any emergency rooms around here. Have you?"

On the surface, it sounds like anger and spite, but Nathan realizes that the true emotions behind Earl's tone of voice are fear and powerlessness.

Fear of ending his days here. And maybe it's even more than that. Maybe it's the fear of being alone when it happens. That the others might choose to leave him behind.

"You've got some foreign body buried in there," Nathan says, again in his *non-negotiating* voice. "Whether it's a piece of the rusty pipe we didn't get out, I don't know. But what I *do* know is that you can start waving goodbye to that leg if we don't do something about it soon. And by *soon,* I mean *today.* Is that clear?"

Earl closes his eyes, shakes his head resignedly, and forms an inarticulate *fucking shit* with his lips.

Then he nods.

CHAPTER 17

"That's the task. Any questions, my Captain?"

Jessie shakes her head, and Nathan nods approvingly.

"Good. Would you mind repeating to me and Meredith what we're looking for?"

"Robert Redbeard's hidden treasure."

"And where did he hide it?"

"A place where there is a cave and different colors of the rocks."

"Exactly. And what do we do if we find such a place?"

"Stay put and call for the others."

"Excellent. And what *don't* we do?"

"Go into the cave."

"Perfect. Now, off with you, Captain."

Jessie smiles and nods, then turns around and runs toward the rocks ahead—and as agreed, she stays within sight.

"And now the real explanation, please," Meredith says, placing a hand on Nathan's shoulder. "What are we looking for?"

"*Escama ferosa*," he replies. "It's a fish that lives in deep-sea trenches around the Galapagos Islands."

"And it's relevant to us because ...?"

"Because its scales are filled with tiny blisters containing a strong poison, which is released if the scales are broken or damaged."

"How strong?"

"Very. If consumed orally, it's deadly to humans. Even in very small amounts, it paralyzes the nervous system within seconds, and you'll be gone before you even realize what happened."

Before continuing, he makes eye contact with Meredith, guiding her attention toward Earl by glancing in his direction.

"However, if instead of drinking the poison, you just apply it to your skin, it's not deadly. Then it has an anesthetic effect that can last for hours."

"Long enough to perform a minor surgery," Meredith says, and Nathan nods.

"Exactly."

"And Redbeard's colored cave?"

"*Escama ferosa* is primarily found in and around hydrothermal vents, which are a sort of underwater fountain where hot water flows out from the ground. And hydrothermal water contains a very high concentration of minerals and salts, which is why deposits are created on the rocks around the vent. Often it'll be some quite beautiful—and very colorful —mineral formations."

"Redbeard's colored cave," Meredith repeats, this time in an *ah, now I get it* tone of voice.

Although Nathan—if he's honest with himself— had to send his inner angels and demons into the gladiator arena before making the decision to spend some of their precious time finding anesthesia for Earl, he quickly realizes that it was a good idea.

For as they walk there, among these huge, dark rocks that stand like giant tombstones in an over-sized cemetery, it's nice to have a goal. Something to distract them from the stench of rotting fish and the eerie, dry sound it makes when seashells and conches occasionally crack under the soles of their shoes.

And from the mental image of the hourglass running out.

The distraction is welcome ... but it doesn't last forever. And when, just over half an hour later, they still haven't come across any colorful mineral formations, a feeling of discouragement begins to sneak in on Nathan. Not only is he worried at the prospect of having to perform surgery on Earl without anesthesia. He's also burdened with guilt for wasting valuable time on nothing. That he may have used his daughter's—

"DAD!" sounds farther ahead. "DAD, HURRY! I THINK I'VE FOUND IT!"

He ought to get angry and scold Jessie because when he looks up, he can't see her auburn hair anywhere. In other words, she has broken the rule of staying within his line of sight.

But it isn't anger that floods Nathan. It's a sense of hope.

He runs in the direction of the sound, rounds the corner of a gray-black rock with a motley collection of sharp tips, and from there continues over to Jessie, who is standing still waiting for him—luckily, she hasn't broken that rule.

A few yards behind her, he sees it. Robert Redbeard's cave. And the brightly colored mineral deposits that mark its entrance leave no doubt in his mind. This is the hole from a hydrothermal vent.

That's still no guarantee of anything, he says to himself, trying to keep a cool head. *It might be empty.*

"Well done, Captain," he says, tousling Jessie's hair as he passes her. "Now, let's see if we got lucky."

He stops at the cave's entrance—a hole in the rock wall about twenty-five inches in diameter—and looks inside.

The first section, like the surface of the entrance, is covered with mineral formations of different colors. Alternating shades of red, orange, and green form a kaleidoscopic pattern. Behind this, the interior of the hole reveals itself as a labyrinth with hidden chambers and narrow passages. The tunnel walls are smooth from countless years of hot water and steam flowing through them. In them run thin crevices that are also coated with minerals, making them look like ores of gold and silver like those found in a mine shaft.

The sight is impressive and, under normal circumstances, the opportunity to study such a vent up close this way would have been a dream come true for a marine biologist like him. But normal circumstances are a thing of the past, which is why Nathan doesn't spend many seconds admiring the cave before he starts looking for the thing that brought him here.

He leans forward and sticks his head into the cave so he can see the back of the thickest layer of the mineral formation. He knows that the *Escama ferosa* likes to build its home there—partly because the stable temperature and nutrient-rich environment in hydrothermal caves contribute to a high survival rate for the fish's offspring, and partly because the same nutrients attract many small fish and crustaceans, which are the adult *Escama ferosa's* primary food source.

And he hits the jackpot. In a crescent-shaped notch behind a pink crystal, it lies; a slender, ink-black fish with thin, elongated scales sitting close to its body and extending backward, almost like the spines of a hedgehog.

As with the rest of the fish of the ocean at present, this one is deceased. Nonetheless, Nathan feels the hairs on his neck rise at the thought of having to approach it. *Handle* it.

He pulls his head back out of the cave, takes the emergency bag off his shoulder, and puts it on the ground, after which he opens it and finds what he needs.

The Swiss Army knife, check.

An empty water pouch, check.

The now empty wine bottle that Jessie found, check.

"What's that for?" Jessie asks as he starts to cut off the top of the water pouch.

"I'm going to use it as a glove to protect my hands when I need to grab the fish."

"You can't touch it with your fingers at all?"

Only if you're willing to gamble with your sense of touch—and possibly your life.

"It's better to be safe than sorry, right?"

When his square plastic mitten is ready, he pulls it over his hand and walks over to the cave, where he leans in once more and then carefully grabs the fish.

It feels slippery. As if it might shoot out of his hand like a wet piece of soap if he squeezes too hard.

"Oh, I forgot the bottle," he says, nodding toward it. "Do you mind taking off the cork and putting it in the sand? Maybe make a small hole so it doesn't tip over?"

Jessie nods, then does just that.

Very carefully, Nathan scrapes the blade of the knife down the side of the fish, gradually applying more and more pressure until the blisters beneath its scales start to burst and a thick, greenish liquid seeps out of them.

As more blisters burst, the strands of the liquid meet and gather into a small stream that runs down to the caudal fin and from there drips into the wine bottle.

Right about an ounce. Enough to kill a handful of larger mammals—and more than enough to put Earl's leg to sleep for an hour or two.

With that thought, Nathan gets back up and tosses the fish back into the cave. Next, he gently pulls off the glove and does the same with it, after which he puts the stopper on the wine bottle.

And then he takes a deep breath and holds it for a few seconds before letting it out in a long, relieved sigh as he—quite literally—shakes off the experience. Once that's done, he walks back to the cave entrance, where he picks out the most beautiful crystal formation—a collection of circular crystal flakes that together resemble the head of a rose—and breaks it off.

With it in hand, he turns to Jessie, who immediately puts two and two together.

"Is that the treasure?"

"The one and only," Nathan says, handing her the crystal. "Robert Redbeard stole the crystal rose from the King of Columbia and hid it here in the cave. It's yours now, Captain. You've earned it."

CHAPTER 18

After weighing the pros and cons, Nathan and the group's other two adults decide that postponing Earl's surgery until they've set up camp for the evening is the most sensible thing to do. Firstly, neither surgeon nor patient is eager to do it in between these obscure and claustrophobic obelisks, and secondly, the campfire will give them another tool for the process as the flames can be used for sterilizing.

So, they clench their teeth, pull on a mask of determination, and march on among the massive rock tombstones of this shady cemetery. Every step requires willpower, every smile even more so, because this part of the trail offers a myriad of unpleasant sights and experiences.

The first is a mound in the sand between two rocks on which lies a large octopus, dried up and lifeless, like some tragic sculpture. Its tentacles, now wrinkled and parched, are entangled and lie limply on the sand all the way around its body like a grisly wreath of death.

As they pass the octopus, Jessie trails it with uncertain, frightened eyes, clutching the crystal flower against her chest with both hands as if it were a teddy bear she was trying to comfort herself with.

She does the same a little later when the lack of a better alternative forces them to walk through a narrow passage whose sandy bottom is sprinkled with the bones of parched sea creatures. Between these, crustaceans of various sizes dash around, their claws raised above them like scorpion tails, ready to sting.

"How long can those bastards stay alive without water?" Earl asks, as one of them grabs his crutch and rides along as he moves it.

"The smaller crustaceans, not that long," Nathan replies. "Three days, maybe. The bigger ones ..."

He finishes the sentence with a shrug, which is the honest answer. He knows that crabs can stay alive without water for a while because they can continue their oxygen intake via their shells, and he also knows that the length of that while depends on the size of the crab ... but what he has no way of knowing is how big the crabs can get down here on the seabed midway between Ecuador and the Galapagos Islands.

"I think we'll soon be out in the open again," Meredith says, pointing.

Nathan follows the invisible line from her fingertip past the next three or four clusters of rocks in their path.

She could be right. For a long time, he's seen nothing but new, dark gray spires when looking behind the nearest rocks in the direction of the horizon. Now, however, there is a view of a blue-white, marbled sky.

Instinctively, and with no need to coordinate with each other, this observation makes all four of them speed up. Even Earl seems to adjust the pace and stagger a tad faster.

In truth, it's a silly impulse, because as long as they are out of water, the shadows are probably their best defense against dehydration. That just doesn't change the fact that moving around in here is eating away at their spirits, and the urge to get out into the light is almost uncontainable.

Ten minutes later, they're finally on their way out. Nevertheless, the gloomy cemetery doesn't let them go until it's given them a final, horrific sendoff. A tiger shark, its body now broken and tarnished, is stuck in a crevice like a gloomy memorial to the once lush sea. Its teeth are exposed as a frightening warning of what could have been—and that they should be glad they were allowed to escape alive.

And they are—at least briefly.

"Oh, hell no! You've got to be kidding me," Earl groans from behind Nathan. "Just give us a fucking chance, already!"

CHAPTER 19

The canyon is enormous and unforgiving. Like an insatiable, gaping mouth, just waiting to tear them apart with the sharp rock teeth that make up its foundation and devour them the second they venture down there.

And they *will* have to go down there. There literally is no way around it. No bridge or trail allows for passage, and there is no end or beginning to be seen in either direction. The canyon is a barrier they are forced to cross if they want to continue southwest.

"Not today," Meredith says in a voice that is hoarse, rasping, and devoid of hope. "I just ... I can't handle any more today."

Nathan, standing on a ledge at the edge of the canyon, replies with a nod, but he doesn't look at her.

His gaze is fixed on what is a few hundred yards below him, down in the abyss.

The darkness. It runs like a river down there. A pitch-black, waterless river.

The valley of death, he thinks, feeling a shiver move down his spine.

Something touches his hand and creeps into its palm. It's Jessie. He doesn't have to look at her to know—and he doesn't feel like doing so right now, as his eyes would give away too much of his true state of mind. So, he settles for closing his fingers around hers and giving them a squeeze.

"Meredith is right," he says, once he's gotten enough control of his emotions to turn around and look his fellow travelers in the eye. "We set up camp here for the night. And we're not having crabs for dinner today. We're gonna take one of the food rations from the bag."

He pauses, waiting to see if anyone will protest and point out that it's smarter to eat the shellfish before they're gone. No one does. The only answer is from Meredith, who folds her hands and holds them up to her chest as if to thank her god.

While preparing to make camp, Nathan discovers that there are a few bright spots after all. One is the location of the campsite, which practically chooses itself. It's a well-sheltered, crescent-shaped notch in a large rock, which has a level floor of sand with plenty of room for both the campfire and their sleeping spots.

The second bright spot is a plant growth on the side of another rock, which is located opposite the notch, approximately thirty feet away. Since this plant is very dense—and grows all the way down to the sand at the foot of the rock—they can use it as a soft support for Earl's back when it's time for the operation.

When it's time for *him* to operate. The mere thought of it makes Nathan's stomach tighten and hurt.

"How much was in it?" Earl asks. "Food, in the bag, I mean. I know you told me earlier, but I can't remember."

Nathan walks over to the emergency bag and zips it open. Next, he places a folded blanket on the ground and starts laying out food rations on it while reciting.

"Six packs of dried fruit and nuts, twelve energy bars with different flavors ... and last but not least; six cans. Three with beans in tomato sauce and three with vegetable soup."

"A freaking feast," Earl says.

Nathan smiles and nods, even though he thinks

to himself that he would trade all of it for a bottle of water in the blink of an eye.

Once they've got the fire going, they sit around it, sharing a bag of dried fruit, while they wait for the contents of the two cans they've chosen—one of each —to start boiling.

And the ship mechanic is right. After living off crab meat for several days, this does feel like a freaking feast, even though they don't have any bowls and are forced to eat directly from the hot cans.

Knowing it's on the verge of gluttony, Nathan ends the meal by handing out energy bars to each of them —and the joy on his daughter's face as she receives one removes any doubt as to whether it's the right decision.

However, like all good things in life, this feast, too, must end, and when the last bit of the energy bar has found its way down to his stomach, Nathan gets up, grabs the emergency bag, and walks over to the vegetation on the side of the other rock to prepare for Earl's surgery.

He starts by spreading out two aluminum blankets. One he places so that half of it lies on the plant and the other half on the sand. The second blanket he spreads out on the ground next to it, after which he places his surgical equipment on it.

The Swiss Army knife, the wine bottle with the anesthetic poison from *Escama ferosa*, one of the empty water pouches, a flare, and some small, dry twigs that he has collected during the day.

As Nathan sits there, staring at his far-from-optimal gear, Meredith approaches quietly. She says nothing; she just stands next to him, patiently waiting, until the urge to put his thoughts into words overpowers him.

"I don't have the faintest clue what I'm doing," he sighs. "What if I end up making it worse?"

"I'm not sure it can get much worse," she replies, placing a steady hand on his shoulder. "What is the flare for?"

"We don't have anything to stitch the wound with, so I figured we could use the gunpowder to seal it. It burns quickly and at a high temperature, and ... to be honest, it's something I've seen people do in movies. I've got no idea if it actually works."

"You should probably leave out that detail when you tell *him* about it," she says, nodding toward Earl.

"I plan to."

After the conversation with Meredith, Nathan goes back to the notch, where Earl and Jessie sit, playing tic-tac-toe in the sand with two small sticks.

"Bedtime, princess."

"Captain," Jessie corrects him without moving her

gaze from the tip of Earl's stick, which is about to foil all of her plans. "Can we finish the game?"

"Okay, but then you have to promise me that you'll go to sleep right away."

Jessie conveys her view on that condition through a sigh of despair but still accepts the agreement and nods.

Half an hour and half a bedtime story later, she has drifted into sleep like a boat on calm water, and Nathan nods to Earl and Meredith, after which all three of them get up and move, as silently as possible, over to the sparsely equipped operating room.

"Will you disinfect this by the fire, please?" Nathan asks, handing the Swiss Army knife to Meredith. He then turns to Earl, who has just taken a seat on the blanket. "Are you sitting comfortably?"

"Better than I have in days," Earl says, nodding back toward the plant that acts as a cushion for his back.

"Good. Then let's get started and get it over with."

With those words, Nathan starts removing the bandage from Earl's leg, exposing the wound on the calf muscle. It looks roughly the same as it did earlier in the day, but the stench has gotten worse. He can almost taste the bitterness of the infection in his own mouth when he breathes.

He grabs the wine bottle with the anesthetic

poison, opens it, and pours a few drops onto the empty water pouch. Then he picks up the pouch and uses it as a makeshift cloth, while gently spreading the green liquid out on the skin around the wound.

Earl frowns but lets him do it—and after a minute or so, it's clear that the poison is beginning to take effect. His breathing gets calmer, and the calf muscle, which before was as hard as granite, gradually softens.

"I'm gonna try to apply a bit of pressure here, okay?" Nathan says, placing his thumbs an inch from the wound on each side. "Let me know if it hurts."

Once again, Earl's face contracts in a tense grimace, but it's the anticipation of pain that triggers it, not the pain itself, and when that dawns on him, he lets out a sigh of relief and smiles.

"And if I do this?" Nathan asks, pressing a little harder.

Another relieved smile from Earl. So far, so good.

On the edge of Nathan's field of vision, a shadow appears. It's Meredith's hand offering him the Swiss Army knife, the blade of which has now turned bluish black after spending time in the campfire.

Nathan accepts it, smiles gratefully at her, and then turns his gaze back to the wound.

"If it gets too bad—"

"Just get on with it!" Earl grumbles.

Nathan nods, wipes cold sweat off his forehead with his sleeve, and then moves the knife up to the wound. There, he lets it hang in the air for a second while exchanging a brief glance with Meredith. Her face is calm and filled with a quiet confidence for which he's deeply grateful.

Carefully, he presses the blade of the knife against the infected flesh, increasing the pressure until there is a squishing sound and the tip sinks through the outer crust. Under the knife, a tiny, yellowish bubble appears, and as he starts to cut, it bursts, sending thin strands of infectious liquid down his leg.

"I think I see the problem," Nathan mutters, partly to himself, partly to the others. "The dark spot, right there. That's the culprit, I think."

"Excellent. Then get it out," Earl orders in a voice revealing that the anesthesia hasn't taken all the pain.

Nathan nods and gets back to work. He makes a cross-shaped cut across the dark spot and then tilts up one of the loose skin flaps with the tip of the knife.

He was right. There's a small strip of rusty metal buried in there. Undoubtedly, it is a remnant of the pipe that caused the wound in the first place.

With the finish line now in sight, Nathan starts

making small cuts on top of each other until he's deep enough in to reach the metal piece—and once he is, he turns to Meredith and hands her the Swiss Army knife again.

"I need to use the pliers in it. Could you give that a round in the fire too?"

Meredith nods and walks over to the campfire with the knife. When she returns, the blade of the knife has been tucked away and a miniature set of pliers has taken its place.

"Thank you," Nathan says as he accepts it. He then looks up at Earl, who sends him more or less the same message as before. This time he's just saying it with his eyes.

Just get on with it!

Nathan does just that. One swift pull, and then he sits with the cursed metal strip that has caused so much damage, jammed between the jaws of the pliers.

Relieved—but also terribly aware that it's not over yet—he pauses briefly to catch his breath. Then he picks up the emergency flare from the blanket and uses the knife to split it open at one end.

"Meredith, can you get me some fire?"

"The lighter doesn't work?"

"Yeah, but I'm not too keen on using that," he

replies, frowning. "It's a storm lighter. Its flame burns too strong. One of those would be better, I think."

Meredith follows his gaze down to the blanket and the small pile of dry twigs, from which she grabs a few and brings them with her over to the campfire. Meanwhile, Nathan begins sprinkling gunpowder from the flare onto the wound.

When she returns, Meredith hands him a twig, the top of which is on fire, making it look like an oversized matchstick. Nathan accepts it, gently blows on the flame to make sure it doesn't go out ... and then slowly moves it down toward the gunpowder.

"You're gonna feel this, okay?"

Earl takes three quick inhalations and exhalations, before squeezing his lips together and giving his consent with a determined nod. However, his lips are forced apart again a second later when the flame comes into contact with the gunpowder.

That Earl screams is no wonder, though. Because what Nathan expected would happen—that the wound would be sealed in a fleeting moment of sparks and smoke—isn't what actually happens.

The wound *is* sealed, yes. But the gunpowder ignites and burns far more fiercely than he had imagined. It only takes a fraction of a second before Earl's entire lower leg—and the bottom of the boiler suit's trouser leg, which is rolled up just above his knee—is on fire.

In a moment of confused desperation, Nathan starts shoveling handfuls of sand onto the leg. Then he realizes that he has a better solution at his fingertips. He grabs the aluminum blanket, throws it over the flames, and grabs around Earl's leg with both arms, enclosing it until the lack of oxygen has suffocated the fire.

When it's over, Nathan instinctively looks back at Jessie, who, by some miracle, has managed to sleep through it all.

Relieved—and exhausted—he releases his grip on Earl's leg and lets himself fall sideways so that he ends up lying on his back on the sand.

"I really didn't think that ... Christ, I'm sorry, Earl," he groans. "Are you okay?"

Earl coughs and blinks in confusion, then pushes the blanket off his leg with slow, meticulous movements.

"I ... think so," he says as he examines the black residue left by the fire in and around the wound. "It hurts like hell, but it looks like it worked."

Nathan pushes himself up on his elbow so he can see. The area around the wound is still red and swollen, and the nasty imprints of the infection remain visible. They probably will be for some time.

But the most important thing is that the surgical wound itself has been sealed—and that the flames didn't have time to melt his skin before they were suffocated with the blanket. Admittedly, most of the hairs on Earl's leg have been turned into small, scorched stubs, but that's a small price to pay.

It would seem that the patient agrees, because now Earl makes eye contact with him and gives him a grateful nod. Afterward, he does the same with Meredith.

"It was a bit too exciting for my taste," Nathan says as he gets up and starts cleaning up the mess. "I'm going to go out like a light as soon as I hit the blanket tonight."

Less than half an hour later, he has proven that claim.

CHAPTER 20

Three draining chemo treatments, two operations, three long-term hospitalizations—and now the prospect of a fourth.

Two years of hell ... and what do the men in the white coats say? Cross the Go square and start over again, Mrs. Bray. That's what they say.

Right now, Michelle is sitting on the couch in the sunroom, alone, staring out at the streetlamps and the snowy rooftops of the town on the other side of the hedge. She often does that.

She's crying. She often does that too. Especially in the evening, right after Jessie is put to bed, like now.

As he reaches the doorway into the sunroom, Nathan sticks his head in and gently taps the frame.

"I'm gonna make a cup of coffee. Do you want one?"

"Yes, please," Michelle replies, rubbing her eyes. "Did you get her to sleep?"

"Yep, Timmy Tortuga's adventures never fail."

He pulls his head back and starts to turn away from the door but then hesitates.

"Sugar or sweetener?"

"What?"

"In your coffee. Sugar or sweetener?"

"Sugar."

Damn it. That means it's one of the bad days.

When returning a little later, Nathan has a cup in each hand. One he places on the coffee table in front of her, and the other he brings with him over to the window, where he stops and stares out across the garden.

"I forgot the icicles on the gutter again," he says, shaking his head. "Can you help me remember it tomorrow? If one of them falls down while Jessie is playing out there—"

"Would you mind sitting down for a minute?"

"Huh?"

Michelle looks at him and repeats her request by patting the couch.

"Oh ... sure, of course," Nathan says hesitantly, after which he walks over and takes a seat next to her on the couch.

"There's something I need to talk to you about."

That phrase—and especially the gravity of her voice

—makes him anxious, and normally it would trigger some stupid remark from him. It's not a character trait he's particularly proud of, but it's just the way he works. This time, however, he manages to stifle that reflex and keep his mouth shut.

"I know you don't want to hear it," Michelle continues —and she's right. He doesn't. "But this will be the fourth time I've had to be hospitalized now, Nathan. And if the treatment doesn't work this time either, then ... then I'd like this to be the last time."

Nathan is silent. Not on purpose, though, because he wants to answer. In fact, he feels like yelling and screaming his answer. He just can't squeeze a single word out through his throat.

"I can't keep doing this, Nathan," she says in a trembling voice. "I won't keep doing this."

Somewhere in the darkness outside the window, a police siren howls and, as always, it triggers a chorus of barking dogs in the neighborhood. Nathan hears them but only as something peripheral and distant. As if they're standing at the bottom of a deep mine shaft and he at its entrance.

"I-I don't understand what you're saying," he stammers. "You don't want to be admitted to the hospital anymore?"

"If it doesn't work this time, I don't want to be treated anymore. That's what I'm saying."

"In the hospital? Then you don't want to be treated anymore ... in the hospital?"

"Then I don't want to be treated anymore, period. No more surgeries and no more chemo. No more time away from my home and my family."

Out in the night, the police car is moving out of earshot, and the siren takes on a distorted, descending tone. The same high-pitched crescendo as when someone imitates the sound of a plane crashing by whistling.

"But ... time away from your family? Are you hearing yourself, Michelle? If you don't get treated, it won't be long before you don't get any more time with us at all!"

"And that's okay," she says with a calm that chills Nathan's spine. *"I'd rather fill the time I have left with good days and good memories than with surgeries and chemotherapy that have no effect anyway."*

Nathan closes his eyes and buries his face in his hands. He needs the darkness behind his eyelids. He needs a moment to pick out the right one from all the potential answers that are swirling around inside his head, knocking into each other like bumper cars in a county fair.

"And what about when it gets worse?" he says, lowering his hands so she can see the anger in his eyes. *"How tough do you think you'll be when the real pain starts?"*

"I don't know," she says. *"But I know I can't go on like*

this. And I also know that when I leave, it's gonna be on my terms."

Nathan is about to ask what the hell that is supposed to mean, but something makes him jump up from the couch instead and leave the sunroom in anger.

Maybe it's the fear that she might have the answer ready at hand.

DAY 4

CHAPTER 21

When he opens his eyes and takes his first conscious breath of the day—through a mouth that feels as parched and coarse as the dusty landscape surrounding him—Nathan Bray is overwhelmed by an almost unbearable sense of discouragement.

It's day number four since the water disappeared from the face of the Earth, and there is no end to their suffering in sight—neither on the physical horizon beyond the canyon nor on the horizon of hope, which is harder and harder for him to call forth when he closes his eyes.

He had expected it to be tough, but he had never imagined anything like this.

He spots Meredith standing at the edge of the canyon, staring into the abyss. Her arms are crossed, her hands wrapped around her elbows as if she's freezing. Behind her, the lower part of her coat dances to the arbitrary rhythm of the wind.

It doesn't take a very well-developed sense of empathy to figure out that she's struggling with some of the same frustrations and worries as him.

With a body that feels like a rusty and creaky engine, Nathan gets up and walks over to her.

"We're not going to make it," she says as she hears him approaching. "Are we?"

"We ... have to keep hoping," he replies in a voice that doesn't even sound convincing to his own ears.

She turns her head and looks at him with narrowed eyes, and for a moment, he's terrified that she is going to say the exact word that he fears hearing.

But Meredith doesn't ask *why* they have to keep hoping. She simply lets her gaze drift over to the notch where Jessie is still sleeping, and then she nods with her eyes turned downward.

"I'm sorry," she says. "You're right, of course. It's just the ramblings of an exhausted old lady. Don't mind me."

Nathan shrugs, sending her a frozen smile.

"What do you say we get the fire going and see if the smell of breakfast can get the two sleepyheads up?"

"I say that's a good idea."

With those words, Meredith walks over to the campsite and starts preparing the fire, while Nathan strolls along the feet of the rocks, checking under loose stones and in small cavities. At least, it's pretty easy to both find and catch crabs. For now.

When he returns with his catch, three medium-sized crabs, Jessie has woken up. She sits with the blanket wrapped around her, watching Meredith work with drowsy eyes.

"Good morning, princess. Did you sleep well?"

Jessie rubs her eyes and nods.

"Yeah ... but I'm so thirsty, Dad. My throat hurts."

Now it's Nathan who, under the pretense that the smoke from the fire is bothering him, rubs his eyes.

"I know, sweetie," he says. "But the food will be ready soon, and it will help to get something in your stomach, don't you think?"

Without giving Jessie a chance to answer—and thus prolonging the conversation—Nathan turns toward Meredith and points down to Earl's sleeping place, which is empty.

"Where did he go?"

"Had to mark my territory," says a deep voice behind him, and when he turns around, he sees Earl come hobbling toward him.

"You look well. How's the leg?"

"Better," Earl says. "Much better. In a day or two, it'll be strong enough for me to give you a kick in the ass for setting me on fire."

He pauses as he staggers the last stretch over to Nathan. Then he places a hand on his shoulder and adds:

"But seriously, thank you, buddy. I owe you one."

"Don't mention it."

"You set him on *fire*?" Jessie exclaims as if Earl's words have only now gotten through to her.

"He's just kidding," Nathan hastens to say. "Right, Earl?"

"Um, yeah ... yeah, of course."

After breakfast, the group gathers their belongings, double-checks the food rations, and packs everything in the emergency bag. Then they walk out to the edge of the canyon and take a moment to mentally prepare themselves for the dangerous descent that awaits them.

This proves difficult because the sight is tremendously intimidating. Spiky and twisted rock formations in ash-gray and black colors dominate the slope, and the ground between these is filled with gravel. Each step will carry the risk of triggering a rockslide, putting them all in danger. It's almost as if they've entered some other world inspired by Mordor from *The Lord of the Rings*.

For a moment, that image is so real to Nathan that he can almost smell the sulfur and hear Sauron's orc army marching in the distance.

"I'm thinking we'll start over there," he says, pointing. "And then follow that one as far as we can."

That one is a groove that twists down the slope, almost like a natural pathway. Whether it can take them all the way to the bottom is impossible to say, as it disappears into the darkness further down. But if nothing else, it can give them a relatively gentle start.

After receiving a nod from Earl and Meredith, Nathan turns to Jessie, who still seems as down-hearted and discouraged as she was when she got up.

"I don't know if astronauts and pirates are gonna cut it today, sweetie," he says. "I think we might need something more powerful. I think maybe ..."

He glances to the sides as if to check that no one is listening before lowering his voice to a whisper and ending the sentence with:

"... we should pull on the capes."

"Superheroes?"

"Nathan Nightfire and Jessie Jawbreaker," Nathan says, widening his eyes as if to say: *Is that cool or what?*

Jessie's lower lip moves as if she's literally tasting the words. Then she approves the proposal with a shrug—and by giving her father's hand a half-hearted slap when he raises it.

The world's least enthusiastic high-five, Nathan thinks as he lowers his hand again and says:

"Excellent, Miss Jawbreaker. Glad to have you on the team. What do you say we help these poor *normal* people cross that gap? If we get it done quickly, maybe we'll have some time to look for a sea turtle afterward."

CHAPTER 22

There isn't any room for blunders or daydreaming on the steep slope. As a constant reminder of this, every step is followed by the crunching sound of pebbles sliding under their weight.

The first part was fairly passable as they had the natural trail in the landscape. But from the moment the trail ended, and its sandy ground was replaced with a carpet of loose rocks, each movement has been a battle against gravity, which won't hesitate to drag them into the abyss if the opportunity arises.

Nathan and Jessie are leading the way. They walk hand in hand ten feet ahead of the others, looking for solid footholds on the untrustworthy surface of the rocks.

So does Earl, who is next in line, except that he uses his crutch to test the stability of the stones.

The backstop is the oldest member of the group, which is also starting to shine through. Because Meredith is tired today. Her face is contorted, and her old legs tremble from the exertion. Nevertheless, she has stubbornly declined every time one of the others has asked if she needs a break.

Before long, however, Nathan intends to insist that they take a rest as he has just spotted the challenge that awaits them farther down. And they will need the energy once they get there.

Ironically, the obvious place for taking a break is also the reason why they will need it.

The rocky outcrop runs across their route, forming a wide ledge that almost looks like the base of a bridge over the deep that just never was finished. Presumably, the protrusion is the result of an underwater earthquake, which would also explain the problematic section right after, where it appears that the entire lower half of the slope has shifted and sunk three or four yards down relative to the rest.

And three or four yards is more than enough when it's an almost vertical descent—and when the ground below is another blanket of unstable rubble.

Now, almost as an eerie extension of that thought, Earl clears his throat and says:

"There will only be one way left after that—and that's down. Because we're not getting back up, that's for sure."

"Honestly, I'm more worried about whether we can even get down there," Nathan says, frowning. "It's too far to jump, and even if it wasn't ..."

He catches himself eyeing Earl's leg and hurries to move his gaze away. But it's too late.

"If you just make sure we keep heading south-west, I'll make sure to keep up," Earl drones.

"Don't worry," Nathan says, demonstratively pulling at the bag's strap to which the compass is attached. At the same time, he double-checks that the red arrow is still pointing in the right direction. For good measure.

Once they get down to the rocky outcrop, Nathan unzips the bag and pulls out two bags of dried fruit. He grabs a handful himself and instructs Jessie to divide the rest equally between herself and the other two. That way she's kept occupied while he gets a chance to look for the best route down from the ledge.

His choice falls on a small, vertical crevice at the outer edge of the outcrop. The texture of its walls isn't significantly different from the rest of the rock's surface, but it has the advantage that the gap between the walls is wide enough to allow them to gain extra support by pushing their hands and feet against both sides.

It will work ... for Jessie and Meredith, he thinks, biting his lower lip. *But you can't ask Earl to push off with his foot, now can you, Professor?*

"Earl, can I borrow your crutch for a moment?"

"I'm assuming you mean my bad-ass *walking stick*?" Earl says with a smile, after which he leans to the side and picks up the plank from the ground next to the rock he's sitting on and hands it to Nathan. "What are you going to do with it?"

"I just need to check something. It'll only take a minute."

With those words, Nathan accepts the crutch and brings it with him over to the crevice, where he gets down on his knees. Then he grabs one end of the plank with both hands and lowers it down the side of one of the walls.

It reaches just under halfway down. That means his estimate of thirteen feet wasn't completely off the mark.

He pulls the plank back up and lays it across so it forms a bridge across the crevice. Afterward, he stands up and steps down on it with one foot. First very gently, then gradually adding more and more pressure.

The plank curves slightly downward under the

weight, but not so much that it's worrying.

Good. It's starting to look like a plan.

Ten minutes later, all four of them stand in a semicircle, staring at the plank. It's still lying over the crevice, and across its middle hangs one of the aluminum blankets, rolled tightly together so that it looks like a thick rope, the ends of which hang in the air on both sides.

"I'm thinking you get the honor of going first, Meredith," Nathan says. "Then you can help Jessie down afterward, and I can stay up here so I can assist Earl."

Meredith looks at him with eyes that are red from fatigue and exposure to the dry dust in the air. Then, without saying anything, she turns her gaze downward and sits down on the edge of the rock crevice. From there, she grabs the two ends of the blanket, gives them a test pull, and takes three quick breaths before she lets herself slide on her butt over the edge.

The plank creaks and shifts slightly to the side, but Nathan instinctively puts a foot on it, and when Jessie sees him doing that, she does the same on her side.

"Press both feet against the wall instead of just the one," Nathan suggests, but Meredith ignores him flatly. That's fair enough, though, as she seems to have her hands full just keeping the blanket and her own body in check so she doesn't spin too much.

"You should be ashamed of yourselves," she says, having found an indentation that she can put her heel in to stop rotating. "Putting a woman my age through something like this!"

"Nonsense," Nathan says. "What are you? Forty-five?"

"Flattery will get you nowhere."

Apparently, it does, though, because now Meredith has reached the end of the blanket rope.

"Now what?"

"Now you take your foot off the wall, so you hang by your arms with your legs pointing down ... and then you let yourself fall."

Even though this instruction isn't new—Nathan gave it even before they placed the blanket on the plank—Meredith sends him a particularly disapproving look before pulling her leg up and letting go of the blanket.

An unpleasant, crunching sound travels up through the crevice, and for a moment, Nathan's brain insists that it could be the sound of bones breaking inside the old woman's thin legs. But then Meredith stands up, kicks away a few of the loose pebbles—where the sound actually came from—and gives him a thumbs-up.

"Outstanding job, Meredith! You're a rockstar," Nathan says, after which he looks at his daughter. "Don't you agree, Miss Jawbreaker? Especially considering that she doesn't have superpowers like us."

"What? Oh, yeah ... she's cool."

"Are you okay, sweetie?"

Jessie nods but not convincingly enough for her father to buy it.

"If it's okay with you, I have something I'd like to test," he says as he bends down and picks up the emergency bag. "You see, I had planned that I would put the strap of the bag around Earl's chest so I could help carry some of the load when it's his turn. But I'd like to test it with a little less weight first. Is it okay if we try it on you?"

Jessie looks at him with an expression that reveals that she's fully aware of what he's up to—and that she appreciates it.

"We can do that."

"Great. Then put your hands up."

After a moment of confusion, Jessie raises her arms above her head, and Nathan brings the strap from the bag down over her. When it's at chest level, he signals her to lower her arms again, and then he leads her over to the edge.

"Start by sitting down. Just like that, yeah. Now

you lean forward and grab the blanket—and don't worry, I've got you with the strap."

Hesitantly, Jessie leans forward while Nathan stays behind her, making sure the strap is tight enough for her to know that he has got her.

"Good. Then you keep a tight grip on the blanket and slide out on your bum, just like Meredith did."

"I can't do it, Dad. What if I can't hold on?"

"Then you use your superpowers," Earl says, and when both Nathan and Jessie give him a perplexed look, he shrugs and adds, "What? You wouldn't name a hero *Jawbreaker* if she didn't have strong hands, would you?"

You would if you were just looking for something that begins with J, like her name, Nathan thinks. But what he says out loud is:

"Of course! Earl is right. You just clench your jaw-breaking fists around the blanket. Then it won't be a problem."

Jessie's gaze wanders hesitantly back and forth between her father and Earl a few times. Then she nods, closes her eyes, and slides over the edge.

For a moment, Nathan almost follows suit, head-first, because he has given her too little wiggle room with the strap. However, at the last second, he manages to slide to his knees—and then all the way down on his stomach—so that he stops his fall.

Now he's lying there, arms over the edge, hands clasped on the bag, looking at his daughter, whose attitude toward the experience has taken a complete U-turn. She's hanging on the strap, smiling from ear to ear as she alternately pulls harder on the blanket and pushes off on the wall with her feet to make herself swing back and forth.

"Not too hard, sweetie," Nathan groans. "I can't hold you, otherwise."

"Sorry, Dad."

"It's okay. Try to see if you can get it to stop swinging and then let your legs hang straight down so Meredith can grab them."

Jessie does as he asks her to, and below her, Meredith positions herself.

There is just one problem.

"She's too short. I can only just reach her feet. It's because of the strap, I think. Can you lower the bag a bit more?"

"My arms are stretched."

"What if you crawl a bit farther out?"

"Then I'll take a head dive."

"You'll have to let go of it," Earl says.

Nathan feels an almost feverish heat rise up inside him. A warmth that consists of equal parts fear and guilt. Using the strap of the bag was his own brain-dead idea, and it only ended up making the situation worse. Moreover, both his shoulders and his upper arms are assuring him that he won't be able to count on them if Jessie needs to be pulled back up.

He looks over at Earl again, then down at Meredith. Both nod with the same message written in their eyes.

"Jessie," he says, making eye contact with her. "I have to let go of the bag. So, it's very important that you hold on tight and hang completely still so the strap goes free of you, okay?"

A hint of anxiety slides across the girl's face, but she quickly gets it back under control—and then she gives her answer by closing her eyes and nodding.

"That's good, sweetie. Then clutch those jawbreakers together. I'll let go in three ... two ... one ..."

He opens his hands and watches—in a moment that his brain somehow manages to show him in slow motion—as the bag falls down along Jessie's back and past her legs. He even has time to think that it goes free.

But then the strap of the bag hits her hip, causing it to whip sideways over her lower legs, locking itself around them.

A second later, the pull comes, and Miss Jawbreaker's grip on the ends of the blanket rope is mercilessly ripped open.

CHAPTER 23

Jessie's eyes, bulging with fear, as she starts to fall. Her fingers, grasping convulsively at nothing as her body tilts backward in the air so it will inevitably be her back and neck that make first contact with the rubble on the ground.

And worst of all; her lips, shaping the word *Dad*.

Powerless and horrified, Nathan sees all these things through the slow-motion filter his brain has placed over his eyes—and for a split second, he knows, without a shadow of a doubt, that *this* is how it's going to end. With the crunching sound of Jessie's cervical spine snapping upon the encounter with the rocky ground.

A wave of dizziness washes over him, dissolving the world into a grayish-white mist. In its wake, the sound indeed follows; a hideous, resounding crunch, amplified by the short distance between the two rock walls of the crevice. It hits his ear canal, as well as his heart, like a blow with a hammer.

His lips shape her name, but it never escapes them, because as the fog clears, he sees her, lying there at the bottom of the crevice.

Unharmed.

She's lying on top of Meredith, who has her arms around her and holds her in a tight embrace.

Meredith is on her back. That's what he heard; Meredith, who threw herself under Jessie to cushion her fall—and who quite literally has taken the painful clash with the granite shards on her back in place of Jessie.

"Are you guys okay?"

Before answering, Meredith gently rolls over on her side and releases her grip on Jessie, who gets up and then helps her rescuer to her feet.

"A little shaken, maybe, but ... we're okay."

"Are you sure?"

"We're okay," Meredith and Jessie repeat in chorus.

"Thank God. Man, that was scary, I ... I don't know how to thank you, Meredith."

"Don't worry about it," she replies, brushing dust off her arms and thighs. "I'm just glad I could contribute for once. Do you need the bag for Earl as well?"

"Huh? Oh, yes, please. Can you throw it up here?"

"Of course, let me just ... no, wait. What is this?"

A moment of silence. Then follows the rapid clicking sound of a zipper being opened, and Meredith's voice returns.

"Oh no, that ain't good!"

"What is it? What's going on?"

"It's the bag. One of the cans got pierced. Everything's covered in tomato sauce."

All things considered, such a minor issue shouldn't trigger more than a shrug and maybe a swear word or two. Especially considering that Nathan, less than a minute ago, was convinced that his daughter had been seriously injured.

But his body is drained, his nerves are worn thin, and his psyche has been pushed to its limit for the fourth day in a row.

And for some strange reason, it's the thought of tomato sauce on the blankets that pushes him to the breaking point.

He rolls off the edge, grinds his teeth together to stifle the angry roar that wants out, and clenches his fists. Next, he starts hammering them into the ground. Like an angry child, he beats away at sand, seashells, and pebbles. On everything that is within his reach.

The skin on his knuckles gets torn, but he doesn't care. Anger and despair have made his hands numb, and he—

Something grabs his forearm. His first impulse is to resist and pull away, but when he turns his head, he stiffens.

It's Earl who has walked over to him. To do so, he has picked up his crutch again, and now he's leaning over it as if he were a wise old monk in a Tibetan monastery. He's also staring at Nathan with the look that one would expect to find in such a monk. A look you can mirror yourself in. And see how irrational and out of control your behavior is.

"You *need* to get a hold of yourself," he whispers, kindly but firmly.

Part of Nathan knows that the ship mechanic is right. Another part of him wants to maintain his anger. To use it as a shield.

"Why?" he hisses. "Why do I *need* to do that? What difference does it make?"

"For her sake," Earl says calmly. "And for your own."

Nathan tries not to, but something forces his gaze to follow along as Earl finishes his sentence by pointing to the crevice—and the sight of it makes the dam burst. His lips start to shake, and icy tears of shame run down his cheeks.

"Earl, I'm sorry. I ..."

"Forget it," Earl says, offering him his hand.

"Is everything okay up there?" Meredith's voice says from the crevice.

"Yeah, we're coming," Earl yells, after which he sends Nathan a questioning look.

Nathan takes a deep breath and nods. Then he accepts Earl's hand and lets himself be pulled up.

CHAPTER 24

Earl's descent, which Nathan had assumed would be the biggest challenge, went surprisingly smoothly. The main reason was that once Meredith had emptied out its contents, they realized that they could use the emergency bag as an extra link between the blanket and the plank. That way, Earl—and later, Nathan—could climb far enough down to reach the ground without having to jump.

Now, in the late afternoon, the emergency bag is back on Nathan's shoulder and its contents have also been put back, after having been scrubbed with sand to remove the worst stains of tomato sauce. The same goes for the plank, which is back in the usual function as a crutch for Earl.

The landscape around them on the slope also

feels as if it has returned to normal after the brief fluctuation at the rocky outcrop. A relatively even incline, filled with dark gray shards, decomposing sea creatures, and sporadic, dying plants. The only noteworthy change is that they're currently walking in a trench that slopes more and more upward on both sides. But that would only have been a problem for them if they were planning to move sideways, along the canyon, which they aren't. They have the same direction as the trench—straight down toward the bottom.

"Are we there yet?"

Jessie's question is possibly the biggest cliché in the history of children traveling with their parents, and she even delivers it with such a self-pitying tone that just a few days ago it would have sent Nathan straight into a fit of laughter.

But now ...

"I don't know, sweetie. Maybe an hour or so."

Jessie responds with a sound that's somewhere between an *okay* and an *oh, man,* but she doesn't complain any further. Perhaps she knows it won't change anything, perhaps she's just too tired.

Nathan is also tired. So much so that he occasionally slips into an almost trance-like state only to wake up from it with a jolt immediately after.

But the fatigue isn't the worst part. This dubious

honor goes to *thirst* and all its nasty side effects.

Headache? Yep.

Dizziness? Yep.

The feeling that his skin is shrinking? You betcha.

Surely there are countless other symptoms on the official list that he doesn't remember ... but he's still pretty sure he's had them all during the day.

"It's actually ironic," Earl mutters at his side.

"What is?"

"This," Earl says, gesturing to his surroundings. "All of it. Me. All my life I've been bragging about all the brilliant shit that the landlubbers missed out on. How life at sea was so much better."

He grabs his forehead and shakes his head. Then he swings his free arm to the side, as if he were an opera singer on his way to the climax of the act, and puts his voice down in a deeper, more solemn tone.

"My home is out there, in the calm and the fresh air. That is where I belong. That was the kind of bull-crap I'd say. The kind of thing I'd use as an excuse to not grow up and start a family. That my *freedom* was too important. What a load of crap! But I got my way, it seems. I'll be buried at sea."

Nathan looks at him, trying to assess whether

this is a breakdown brewing or Earl just needs an outlet for his frustrations. Thankfully, it seems to be the latter.

"How long have you been working on the ship?"

"Huh? Oh, well, I was permanently employed on *MS Darwin* in 2012 or 2013. Before that, I spent many years working for a shipping company in Guayaquil, but it got too impersonal for me. There were far too many ships ... or rather, too many *crews*. I never got to feel like part of the family like I did on *Darwin.*"

Part of the family. Only now, hearing it phrased that way, does Nathan appreciate what a terrible burden Earl must have been carrying around for the past four days. He has been so focused on himself, on the fact that he's trapped down here with his daughter, that he hasn't really thought about the fact that Earl lost his entire family when *MS Darwin* plunged into the abyss.

He turns toward Earl to correct that mistake but immediately loses focus when he sees him standing, leaning against the crutch with one leg raised, staring at his shoe.

"Fucking gross. What the hell is that?"

As he speaks, Earl reaches his free hand down to his shoe, but Nathan grabs his wrist and stops him.

"Don't touch it," he says, leaning down so he can

take a closer look at the gooey pink lump hanging under the sole of his shoe.

"What is it? A jellyfish?"

"*Pelagia noctiluca*," Nathan says, nodding to himself. "It's a jellyfish, yeah. A real nasty one."

He bends down, picks up an oblong rock, and uses it to scrape the sticky animal off Earl's shoe.

"You can recognize them by the bell shape and the small blisters on their tentacles that make them glow in the dark. They're pretty common in the waters around here, but ..."

He stops mid-sentence and turns to look around.

"But what?" Earl asks.

"Even though *Pelagia noctiluca* don't travel in swarms, they still tend to form groups because they drift with the ocean currents," Nathan says. "And when I say groups, I mean *large* groups."

He doesn't elaborate further and doesn't need to. He can tell by Earl's facial expression that he both understands—and feels—the disturbing premonition.

Soon after, as they reach the top of a mound in the trench, it's confirmed.

In front of them—as a final barrier between them and the floor of the canyon which has now finally come into view—they lie, scattered across the slope.

Thousands of slimy, pink jellyfish.

And millions of almost invisible but very poisonous threads.

CHAPTER 25

"It's *not* the same, Dad. And you know it."

Yes, Nathan knows. When they played *The Floor is Lava* at the fish shoal a few days ago, the biggest risk of a misstep was that their shoes and pants would get to reek of fish. Now, a wrong step is potentially very dangerous.

"Can't we go around it?" she asks in an imploring tone that pierces his heart.

"I'm sorry, sweetie," he says, drawing her attention to the two huge slopes of rubble that make up the sides of the trench. "We would have to go all the way back to the start to do that. It's too far."

"But ... it's *jellyfish*," Jessie says as if that one sentence explains everything—which in a way it does.

Because although Jessie shares her father's love for the ocean and its animals, there is one clear exception. It has a simple reason, though, as Jessie accidentally swam into a jellyfish's threads on a trip to the beach a few years ago. It was an experience that left her with a modest scar on her back and a larger one on her soul.

"Listen, princess," he says, placing both hands on her cheeks. "You'll make it through this, and you know why?"

Jessie sniffles and shakes her head.

"Not because you're an astronaut or a pirate or a superhero," Nathan continues. "But because you're Jessie Bray. My awe-inspiring, butt-kicking daughter who can handle anything the world throws at her."

He leans forward, making their foreheads touch each other, and whispers:

"Can I tell you a secret?"

She nods.

"Without you, I would never have gotten this far."

That is the pure, unspoiled truth. Maybe Jessie can sense that in his voice because when he pulls away from her again, he can see that the edginess in her eyes has disappeared. It has been replaced by a determination that makes her look much older. And a bit like her mother.

"Are we going to make it?" he asks, holding up his hand.

"We'll make it," she says, giving it a slap.

Spotting the jellyfish from a distance was bad enough, but stepping in between them, Nathan realizes right away, is far worse. Because up close they're even more hideous. Their half-dissolved, pink bodies are squashed together and, in many places, intertwine with each other. It's as if they are trying to transform into one giant animal that intends to spread like a large membrane over the entire area. A thick, soupy layer like the one often found on the surface inside cans of preserved food.

But the worst part isn't the pink soup. The worst part is all the thin, poisonous threads, which are undoubtedly spread all over the place ... but which they can't see.

"It's very slippery here, so hold on tightly to my hand, okay? And be sure to only step on the flat stones."

Jessie doesn't answer, but he feels her grip on his hand tighten.

Carefully, he takes the next steps down the slope. It's steeper than he'd like it to be, but apart from that detail, it's going okay.

"Are you with me?"

"We're with you," Meredith replies.

"On the verge of throwing up," Earl adds. "But yeah, still with you."

Because of Jessie, Nathan doesn't say it out loud, but he agrees. It's nauseating to trudge around in this. The squelching sound especially makes his stomach turn. No matter how careful he tries to be when lifting his feet, it's there. Like the sound of a wet and greasy lump of clay being squashed between two hands.

As they approach the last fifteen feet of the barrier, Jessie's grip on Nathan's hand gets tighter and tighter. This, however, isn't a great mystery to him since the last stretch is also the most complicated. There is a depression that runs all the way across the trench. It's about six feet wide at its narrowest point, so it's not that bad ... at least not for adult legs. But for seven-year-old Jessie, six feet is far too great a distance to cover with one jump. Especially when the depression is filled to the brim with jellyfish soup.

After considering the pros and cons in his head for a moment, Nathan takes the bag off his shoulder and turns to face Meredith.

"Would you mind holding this while I get Jessie over? You can throw it to me afterward."

Meredith casts a quick glance down at Jessie,

whose face is still warped in an agonizing expression. Then she nods and accepts the bag.

"You can go ahead and jump up, Lady Bray, knight of the triangular table," Nathan says, squatting down in front of Jessie. "Your trusty steed is ready to transport you across the river."

He supplements his words with his best imitation of a neighing horse, causing Jessie to let out a sound that could be a giggle.

She leans against his back and puts her arms around his neck.

"Are you ready?" he asks, grabbing her wrists so she doesn't end up shutting off his airways when he stands up.

"I'm ready, Draft Wind."

"Draft Wind? Your horse's name is Draft Wind?"

"My horse's name is Draft Wind."

"Fair enough. Then hold on, Lady Bray, because we're saddling up now."

With those words, he pushes himself up, and once back on his feet, he moves his hands down under Jessie's knees and pulls her legs forward so they come to rest on his forearms.

"Are you sitting all right?" he asks, bouncing her up and down slightly as if he wants to check just that.

"Yep."

"Good."

His plan is to get it over with as quickly as possible. Tear off the patch in one swift pull so the agony isn't drawn out. Therefore, he doesn't count down or give any other kind of warning before he takes two quick steps forward and jumps.

He probably should have, because the shock makes Jessie react instinctively. And her way of reacting is to pull her arms backward ... so they end up blocking Nathan's line of sight.

The result is that he can't see anything. So instead of landing on the dry, flat rock he had targeted, his right foot ends up on one whose surface is coated with the slippery body of a half-disintegrated jellyfish.

From the moment he feels his heel find ground and then lose it again, Nathan has only a split second to react. Yet, he somehow manages to shift his weight and spin around so that, instead of landing on his side, he lands facing the ground.

In other words, he ensures that it's *his* face and *his* hands that come into contact with the poisonous threads of the *Pelagia noctiluca*.

CHAPTER 26

"GET HER OFF! GET HER OFF!" Nathan hears himself weave into the steady stream of pain-filled screams that pour out of his mouth. "GET JESSIE OFF!"

Earl and Meredith could've already taken her off him. The truth is, he has no idea because he can't feel his back at all. He can only feel his face and hands. How they burn and sting. How his skin feels like it's melting.

In front of his face, the rubble starts to move ... no, it's him. *He* is moving. Something is making him do it, lifting him and dragging him away.

The pieces fall into place as he registers movement at both extremes of his field of vision. Women's shoes on the left side, safety shoes, and the lower part of an old, worn plank on the right.

"J-Jessie?" he stammers.

"She's safe," Meredith replies from the bottom of a mile-deep well. "You took it all."

Nathan opens his mouth to express his relief, but before he manages to articulate a single word, the rock shards in front of his face begin to liquefy and run together, gradually forming an oil-black pool that slowly but surely consumes everything.

When he wakes up again, it's no longer rubble that he's staring at but the faces of his fellow travelers. All three of them are watching him with the same worried expression in their eyes.

And in Jessie's eyes, there's more than just that. In them are tears.

With difficulty—and eventually a little help from Meredith—Nathan pulls himself up into a half-sitting position, then lets his gaze drift to the ground between Earl and Jessie.

Two things catch his attention. One is that the rocks are dry. Ergo they must have gotten him out of the jellyfish's soup. The second thing is the Swiss Army knife next to Earl. Its blade is extended, and it's smeared in a sticky, pink mass.

Instinctively, he raises his hands and studies them, turning them from side to side.

Red, swollen lines crisscross them—and strangely enough, the pain seems to increase when he looks at them.

"We scraped it off as best we could," Meredith says. "But the pain will linger for some time, I suppose."

"Does it hurt a lot?" Jessie asks.

Nathan opens his mouth, intending to lie to calm her down, but he's caught in it even before the first word has come out because the mere act of moving his lips triggers an intense, fiery pain that ascends his cheeks and brings tears to his eyes.

"It ... hurts pretty bad, yeah," he admits. "But the poison isn't lethal, so I'll be okay."

He glances around again, this time looking for something specific, and when he sees the emergency bag, he points to it with a quivering finger.

"The wine bottle?" Earl asks, and when Nathan nods, he adds, "We considered it, but we were afraid to use too much."

"Give it to me, please," Nathan moans.

Earl nods, then opens the emergency bag, takes out the wine bottle, and hands it to Nathan.

With hands that feel like they're covered in frantic, stinging wasps, Nathan lifts the bottle, looks at the contents behind the glass ... and breathes a sigh of relief. There is still plenty left of *Escama ferosa's* viscous, green poison.

He pours a couple of drops onto his palm and quickly hands the bottle back to Earl. Next, he gently starts to rub the poison on his hands, forearms, and the sorest areas of his face.

Then he waits.

"It isn't working at all?" Jessie asks, seeing tears begin to roll down his cheeks.

"No, no, sweetie," he says, sniffling. "It works perfectly. That's why I'm crying."

CHAPTER 27

The bottom of the canyon is at the same time majestic and miserable. *Majestic* because it's so huge, so intrusive—like a dark gray version of the Grand Canyon stretching across the desolate, parched seabed. *Miserable* because it's now nothing more than a faint echo of the intriguing world it once contained.

The *life* it once contained.

In many ways, it feels like standing in the ruins of a war-torn city, surrounded by shattered dreams and demolished homes. Here it just isn't buildings that have been cleared of life, but the many large caves in the cliffside, which before were masked by the ocean's blanket of darkness.

You can almost hear the desolation of the caves. A faint hissing sound. Like a hoarse, ghostly laugh.

As they sit around the fire waiting for the vegetable soup to boil, these are the sort of gloomy, philosophical thoughts that roam in the back of Nathan's mind.

Conversely, they should probably consider themselves lucky that the caves aren't full of life. They are deep down at the bottom of the sea, after all. So deep that there may well be things down here that Nathan, despite his field of expertise, has never seen or heard of.

A shiver runs over his neck at that thought, and he instinctively puts his arm around Jessie, who is sitting next to him.

"Are you tired, sweetie?"

"Not really, it's more that I'm hungry ... and thirsty. How are you doing?"

"You're so sweet," he says, kissing her hair. "And thank you, I feel much better. It will be completely gone by tomorrow, I think. But I might have gotten some pretty cool scars."

He raises his hand and turns it to show just how cool they are, but it's clearly too soon for the girl to joke about, so he quickly lowers it again.

"We didn't find any sea turtles," Jessie says.

"No, not today, but ... but we won't give up. We'll try again tomorrow, okay?"

"Food's ready," Earl says, and Nathan—eager to change the subject—hurries to pull his sleeves out over his hands and accept the hot can of soup.

He succeeds in changing the subject ... in a way. Because even though he and Jessie don't talk anymore about their failed search for a sea turtle during the meal, it stays in the back of his mind for the rest of the evening.

And when he wraps himself in his blanket—and its bittersweet aroma of tomato sauce—and closes his eyes, it's still there.

The sea turtle. His promise.

CHAPTER 28

"Are you out of your mind?"

Under normal circumstances, asking such a question to your partner is rarely more than a rhetorical attack. A provocation, used as lighter fluid for the flames of anger when a discussion is about to turn into a fight.

That's only partially the case this time as part of Nathan means what he's saying quite literally. Part of him wants to know if his wife actually has lost her mind. Because more and more often, it feels like Michelle is a complete stranger. As if some invisible force has pushed her usual happy-go-lucky spirit out of her body and assigned a bitter, life-weary replacement to take its place. A stranger with whom he tries to communicate, but who doesn't speak the same language as him at all.

At this moment, especially, it's an eerily fitting metaphor, since Nathan finds it hard to understand the words she has just said to him—and even harder to accept them.

"I'm serious, Michelle," he says. "Have you gone insane? You must be to say something like that!"

From her spot in the hospital bed, she stares at him with a look that is close to pushing him over the edge into a fit of rage. Because the eyes in her pale, anguished face show no signs of anger or defiance. More than anything, they look sad—but on his behalf. As if she pities him for taking so long to realize that she, obviously, is right.

"It's not like I'm asking you to do it," she says as if that was supposed to make it better somehow. "All I ask for is your blessing, Nathan. That's it."

"My blessing? You w-want ..."

Halfway through the sentence, his voice loses its strength so that the last few words are never articulated.

For a while, Michelle says nothing. She just sits there, reclined in her bed, while the monotonous beeps of machines fill the semi-dark room. Then she leans to the side, reaches her small, bony hand over to the bedside table, and pulls out the drawer. From it, she picks up a little white pill bottle and places it on the countertop.

BENZODIAZEPINE it says on the label.

"Sleeping pills," she explains. "According to the internet, it's one of the most effective and ... pleasant ways to do it."

"According to the internet?" Nathan repeats, and straightaway he's struck by a terrible insight.

She has researched it. She's actually been sitting with her smartphone or at a computer at some point, spending time looking for the best way to take her own life—which must mean that ...

"You're being serious?"

She gulps with an audible click and nods, but her gaze doesn't fall downward in shame afterward. As it fucking should do. She just stares at him calmly. He, on the other hand, must keep all the muscles of his face in tight reins for it not to crack completely.

"But you ... why, Michelle?"

"Because I can't do it anymore," she says. "I don't have the strength to keep fighting. Not physically, not mentally. Besides, there is no point in fighting anymore. You know that too. All the doctors have given up ... so why can't I?"

Nathan's throat narrows, and his mouth becomes bone dry as if he hadn't had a drink in days. He tries to swallow, tries to clear his throat, tries to cough, but nothing works. His pharynx is closed, strangled by the pressure of the invisible hands that grasp it.

A wave of dizziness and nausea floods him, and he leans forward. Like that he stays, sitting on the edge of his chair, his eyes closed and his head down between his *knees, until the room has stopped tilting back and forth like a ship's deck during a storm.*

Then he lifts his head—and lets out a startled gasp.

Michelle has kicked off her duvet. Now she sits with one leg outstretched on the mattress and the other pulled up to her chest.

It's this bent leg that her hands are clutching. Except that they aren't holding it, but rather tearing and ripping at it. Pulling off strips of rotten, bluish-black skin, digging her nails into the infected flesh so that the big, inflamed blisters burst and a glistening, yellowish liquid seeps down her hands and her shins.

She doesn't even notice. She just continues to tear, rip, pull, twist, and slash until the mattress below her is completely soaked by—

"OH GOD NO! NATHAN, WAKE UP! WE HAVE TO HELP EARL! WAKE UP, NATHAN!"

DAY 5

CHAPTER 29

After being torn out of his nightmare by Meredith's panicked cries, it takes a few seconds for Nathan to make sense of the events unfolding before him.

Part of the reason is that his eyes have to get used to the semi-darkness as the only sources of light are the glow of the moon and a few stubborn embers from the dying campfire.

Another part of the reason is that his otherwise extensive knowledge of marine animal species offers him no help identifying these two.

Their stalked eyes, jointed backs, and large, serrated claws echo the features of lobsters, but if that is indeed what they are, these are far bigger than any lobsters Nathan has ever heard of. Because they're large. So large that they would match his height, or possibly even surpass it, if they were able to stand upright on the back two of their ten legs.

The third—and most important—reason Nathan's brain has suffered a temporary meltdown is that he's in shock. He's simply so frightened by what the animals are doing that he's unable to move.

But he can see. He can see their claws burrowing into Earl's infected calf muscle, ripping off large chunks of meat. And he can hear. Although it ought to be impossible because it's drowned out by the screams of Earl, Meredith, and Jessie, he can hear the squishy, smacking sound as they throw bloody pieces of flesh into their disgusting mouths and chew them.

Something grabs his arm, and for a split second, he's convinced it's another one of those terrifying lobster creatures that has crept in on him unnoticed.

It isn't. It's Meredith. An eerie, distorted version of her, so steeped in horror that her face looks bent and warped. Like an abstract painting.

"WE HAVE TO HELP HIM!" she chants, shaking Nathan's arm as if she were still trying to wake him from sleep. "WE HAVE TO HELP EARL!"

"Get Jessie away from there," Nathan says, after which he, without shifting his gaze from the disgusting lobster monsters, tumbles up into a crouching position. Then he slowly starts moving the opposite way around the fire, keeping it as a barrier between them and him until he has gotten all the way over behind Earl's back.

The monstrosities don't seem to register his presence at all, and neither does Earl, for that matter. He's too busy screaming and trying to pull away from them. He kicks at them too, but it doesn't look like there's much power left in his legs. It has probably leaked out along with the large amount of blood pooling on the ground beneath him.

The crutch lies to the left of Earl. That's what Nathan wants to get his hands on. The problem is that it's also lying very close to one of the monsters. So close that three of its legs occasionally step on it —with a horrible *cla-cla-clack* sound—as it leaps forward to rip another chunk off the ship mechanic's leg.

With the sound of his own pulse rumbling in his ears like a freight train, Nathan stares at those repulsive, serrated spider legs—and as soon as he sees them move backward, he leaps forward.

Barely have his fingers closed around the plank before the animal finally notices his presence. It locks its small, stalked eyes on him, lets go of the raw, torn-apart lump of meat in its claws, and utters a rattling wheeze.

In the blink of an eye, it shoots forward toward

him, claws lifted and clicking, legs ticking away like the needle in a sewing machine.

Nathan takes a swing with the plank, but he hasn't gotten a proper grip on it yet, and although he hits the front legs of the animal's right side, the blow is only enough to push it off balance temporarily. A second later, it's back on offense with the claw shears jabbing relentlessly at his legs as he staggers backward, constantly tripping on loose rocks.

He attempts to kick it, but it results in nothing other than the monster grabbing his pant leg and tearing a hole in it.

He kicks again, this time higher—and even though it wasn't his plan, the result is much better this time as he hits one of the animal's eyes and breaks the stem that holds it up.

The creature lets out an eerie, gurgling cough and starts clawing wildly in the air with feverish and seemingly random movements ... which makes Nathan realize something vital: the animal has lost its sense of coordination.

He grabs the plank, lifts it up—and brings it down on the crustacean.

The first blow causes the animal to hiss again. The second blow causes it to squirm and run in circles, while its hind body twitches up and down.

The third blow causes its jointed back to crack with a crunching sound.

It's dead. Yet it takes all of Nathan's willpower to suppress the urge to keep pounding away at it. But he has to because he still has the creature's mate to think about.

He turns around—and lets out a gasp.

Earl is lying on his stomach with one cheek flat against the ground, swinging his arms from side to side, trying to find something to grab. His left hand is colored a dirty black, as if at some point he has had it buried in the ashes—and the last, glowing pieces of coal—from yesterday's campfire, perhaps hoping to find something in there that he could use to pull himself to safety.

Earl's pursuer is no longer interested in his infected leg. Instead, it has shifted its focus up to his back, where it has cut its way through both the blue fabric of the boiler suit and Earl's pale skin.

Dash forward, cut, and rip. Pull back, chew, and gurgle. Dash forward, cut, and rip. Pull back, chomp, and chew.

Relentlessly—and with an eerie, almost rhythmic precision—the crustacean monster follows this pattern, gradually digging deeper and deeper into Earl's back.

"LEAVE HIM ALONE!" Nathan screams, swinging the plank at full strength into the side of the animal so it rolls sideways across the rocky ground and lands on its back, halfway lying on a rock.

Attempting to turn itself around, the lobster starts squirming violently, while all ten legs twitch back and forth, thrashing against each other's hard shells with the same *cla-cla-clack* sound its buddy made when stepping on the plank.

Fueled by anger and desperation, Nathan raises the plank above his head with both hands, after which he leaps forward and drives its end down with such force that it penetrates the shell—and the monster's belly.

The creature curls up and twists in pain as its guts, a treacly egg-white liquid, are squeezed out between the cracks in the shell.

Nathan sets his foot down on three of its legs and simultaneously twists the plank to the side. More entrails pour out as the monster, perhaps in a final, desperate attempt at resistance, lifts its left claw and opens it. However, instead of closing around Nathan's ankle, the claw only trembles for a moment before falling limply back to the ground.

And as it lies there, Nathan notices an eerie detail. It sits right at the joint where the two sides of the claw meet; a piece of fabric that used to be white, but over the last few days has become so dirty that it's light brown.

Bandage.

He lets go of the plank and turns around.

Earl is still lying on his stomach next to the fire, but he's not alone anymore. He's joined by Meredith and Jessie, both clearly struggling to hold back their own nervous breakdown while trying to comfort him.

As soon as she sees Nathan approaching, Jessie jumps up and throws herself into his arms. He hugs her, kisses her hair, and tells her he loves her.

But he doesn't say that everything is going to be all right.

Not this time.

CHAPTER 30

There are several indicators. Earl's face, which due to loss of blood has been drained of color and left as a chalk-white death mask, is one. His voice, which has lost all its power so that every word forced out between his chapped bluish lips sounds like the last exhalation of a dying man, is another.

Plenty of small indicators. But for Nathan, there's one that expresses it clearer than anything else, and that's the look Earl has had in his eyes ever since they got him up after the night's onslaught. It's the stare of a man who waits for one thing only. The arrival of the Grim Reaper.

Nathan knows that stare all too well.

Above them, the pale light of dawn has begun to

oust the darkness from the sky, but down in the canyon the shadows still prevail. What little light there is only manages to create a weak, faded glow that merely emphasizes the gloomy state of the canyon.

Hopefully, the light will still have a comforting effect on Jessie and Meredith, who sit across from Nathan, on the other side of the fire, and haven't closed an eye since the night's incident. And on himself, for that matter.

That thought leads his gaze down to the dial of his wristwatch. Three hours. That's how long they've been sitting here, three fatigued people with red eyes that constantly wander uneasily back and forth between the dark caves over the cliffside and the corpse-pale face of the ship mechanic, silently awaiting the inevitable.

"Do ... we ... have ... any ... water ... left?"

The hoarse, rasping—and not least *unexpected*—sound of Earl's voice startles Nathan to such an extent that he's about to tip backward.

"Sorry, what?"

"Do we ... have ... any ... water ... left?" Earl repeats.

For a few seconds, Nathan doesn't know what to say, because he's unsure if, in a moment of clarity,

Earl has decided to pull his leg. Then he notices the feverish drowsiness in Earl's eyes and realizes that it's a serious question. That he must have forgotten or perhaps suppressed the fact that they ran out of water yesterday.

"I'm sorry," Nathan replies. "We don't have any water, but we have a bag of dried fruits left. I could find some raisins for you. You liked those, didn't you?"

Earl moves his head slowly up and down.

"Just a sec," Nathan says, after which he leans back and pulls the emergency bag toward himself. "I'll find you some."

He opens the bag, finds the bag of dried fruits, grabs some raisins from it, and hands them over to Earl.

Earl opens his hand so Nathan can put them in his palm, but after that he does nothing. He doesn't close his hand again, nor does he move it up to his mouth. He just stares blankly at—or rather, *through* —the raisins, without doing anything.

Nathan considers taking his hand and helping him, but he decides not to. Earl doesn't seem to remember either his thirst or his hunger anymore.

Once he's put the bag of dried fruits back, Nathan grabs the zipper of the emergency bag and starts closing it. Halfway into the movement, however, he stops as he spots something else in the bag.

The wine bottle. The one that had the letter inside but now contains a bit of *Escama ferosa's* deadly poison instead.

Still with his thumb and forefinger locked around the zipper's strap, Nathan lets his gaze wander up to Earl's pale, sweat-glistening face, and from there over to Jessie and Meredith. Then he closes his eyes—and the zipper.

A little over half an hour later, it happens. Earl Gibson takes one last, labored breath and closes his eyes for the last time, still without having eaten a single one of the four raisins in the palm of his hand.

Meredith and Nathan both see it happen, and when it's over, they exchange a brief glance. Neither of them says it out loud, but Nathan is pretty sure they share the same ambivalent emotions. Sadness, but also relief.

For obvious reasons, Earl doesn't get a coffin six feet underground, nor does he get a lengthy eulogy. He'll have to settle for an aluminum blanket and the fact that he got to end his days at sea, like he always said he wanted.

Nathan is the one who puts the blanket over him. And as he pulls it up to cover the last part of Earl's face, he's struck by a realization that causes a chilling sensation to run through him.

Do we have any water left?

Those were Earl Gibson's final words in this world.

CHAPTER 31

At 3:43 p.m. on the same day, the last three survivors of *MS Darwin* are fighting their way up a particularly vile section of their route up from the canyon.

Not only is it steep as hell on this part of the slope, but the ground is also extremely unstable because it consists of a mixture of pebbles and dry sand. Several times they have been forced to get down on all fours and crawl, just to find enough support.

Every time this has happened, the same thought creeps into the back of Nathan's mind: What if they just stopped moving and stayed there on the ground? Closed their eyes like Earl and allowed themselves to be enveloped in the perfect darkness of death. Allowed their screaming, tormented muscles to rest as they surrendered to the deepest, dustiest library silence and let go of all worries. What would that be like?

The answer—which, without exception, has triggered a chill and a wave of shame in him every time —is always the same. It would be weakness and it would be hypocrisy, born of egocentricity. Pure madness.

But Nathan isn't the only one who's toyed with the idea. Meredith's eyes have revealed that secret to him on several occasions.

"We'll soon be past the worst part," he says to Jessie, who is moaning and groaning a few feet in front of him.

She hasn't asked, nor is she answering. She just continues to stare down at her feet in silence, as she has done most of the day. Even earlier, when they walked in a less steep area and he carried her in his arms for a while, he didn't get more than one-syllable words out of her.

Given the circumstances, though, her silence is understandable. She was woken up at shit o'clock last night to the sight of monsters that only ought to exist in nightmares. A few hours later, she saw Earl pass away. Oh, and don't forget, she's still trapped in a rocky desert without as much as a drop of water.

If that list of things can't discourage a seven-year-old girl, what can?

So yeah, it's perfectly understandable that Jessie needs to withdraw into herself and process it all. And Nathan really should just leave her alone and give her the space to do it. He knows that very well.

But.

"Whoa! Look what I found!"

Jessie looks at him as he bends down to pick up an object between the gravel, but it seems to be more out of courtesy than anything else—and when he hands it over to her, she doesn't accept it. She just wrinkles her nose as if to say: *Nah, you just keep it.*

"It's a fossilized starfish," Nathan says in a tone of voice he realizes is far too eager. "Isn't it beautiful?"

"Yeah, it's pretty," Jessie replies, shrugging indifferently.

"I think so," he says, brushing sand off it with his fingertip. "You're welcome to have it if ..."

She is already gone. It's her back he's talking to. God damnit.

He looks down at the starfish in the palm of his hand, and suddenly it doesn't seem beautiful at all. On the contrary, it looks miserable. Like a tiny art sculpture that symbolically reflects the parched, lifeless world surrounding them.

He closes his hand, turns around, and hurls the

starfish toward the bottom of the canyon. Down to all the other dead beings.

Down to Earl.

"Give it time," Meredith softly advises him from behind. "She'll be okay."

She means well, of course, but Nathan still has to bite his lip not to roar something along the lines of: *Oh, time? You don't say? How long should I give her then? Because my best guess is that we have one, perhaps two days left before we wither and die.*

What he ends up doing is shrugging his shoulders and nodding before following in his silent daughter's footsteps up the slope.

An infinity later, they've finally gotten far enough up the canyon's side to feel the sun's rays on their skin. However, they only manage to get a couple of minutes of its warm embrace before the big, glowing ball turns its back on them again and pulls out of sight somewhere up behind the edge—and by the time they've made it the rest of the way up, it has already passed the baton to its blue-white twin.

It's under her delicate glow that the three travelers—discouraged, beaten, and *very* thirsty—set up camp, less than fifty yards from the edge of the abyss where the fourth member of their group ended his days.

This evening there is no campfire because none

of them have the energy to make one. For the same reason, there isn't any warm food. The menu consists of the sad scraps they have left in the emergency bag. A quarter bag of dried fruit and two energy bars— not exactly enough to cover the needs of three people who have spent the entire day climbing a rocky slope.

And yet it's liquids all three of them crave. Oh man, what Nathan wouldn't do for a bottle of cold water. The thought alone makes his throat burn and his stomach shrink, as if his internal organs are about to implode.

"Do you want me to tell you a bedtime story?" he asks as Jessie lies down in her sleeping spot.

"No thanks. I just want to sleep."

Following this short answer, she pulls the blanket up until it almost covers her entire head and rolls over on her side with her back to him.

"We'll ... find some more food tomorrow," he whispers, stroking his hand over her shoulder. "Some *better* food. I promise."

"Sure, Dad."

He opens his mouth to say something more, like *I'll keep you safe* or *we have to keep hope alive*, but all that comes out is an anguished sigh, as dry as the wind that caresses his neck.

For the next while, silence reigns. For Nathan, it's

the lack of words that causes it. He has simply run out, and he assumes the same goes for Meredith. However, he soon realizes that the reason for her silence is different—because as soon as Jessie has fallen asleep, Meredith clears her throat and, in an eerily calm and serene voice, states that:

"Tomorrow will be my last day."

All the doctors have given up ... so why can't I?

"Listen, Meredith, I know today has been hell, but we—"

"And it's okay," she continues as if he hadn't said anything at all. "I've had a good life and I'm ready. Ready to see my George again."

She hesitates for a moment, sporting the kind of smile that people get on their lips when a pleasant memory surfaces in their consciousness.

"Who knows?" she says. "Maybe a year up in Heaven has cured his fear of heights, so I can finally get him on a plane. Go for an adventure."

"Meredith, that's ..."

A long pause, then a sigh.

"... a nice thought."

"It is, isn't it?" Meredith replies. "I think so too. And I'd be grateful if it didn't become a big thing when I say goodbye."

For a moment, it's unclear to Nathan what Meredith means, but then he sees her glancing over at Jessie, and that makes the pieces slide into place.

"I'll do what I can," he says, nodding.

Meredith intertwines her hands, holds them in front of her mouth, and bends her head slightly forward. It's nothing more than a way of saying thank you to him, but still, that gesture makes the hairs on his neck stand up.

For as this old woman sits there, her hands folded as if in prayer and bathed in the dusty, blue light of the moon, she looks like something taken out of a religious work of art. The kind of woman you'd expect to find at the foot of Jesus on a mural in a Roman cathedral.

Except, of course, for the background, which in this case isn't a lush landscape or the city of Galilee, but rather a dark, weathered wasteland that the Savior will have to visit very soon if He wants to do it, while there is still somebody alive to wave palm branches when He arrives.

CHAPTER 32

All the doctors have given up ... so why can't I?

In the three days since Michelle asked him this question, it has been circling in the back of Nathan's mind like a malicious mantra.

And sometimes, the echo of words can hurt just as much as the words themselves. He's learned that the hard way.

Three days. The same amount of time that has passed since he last visited her in the hospital. He neither can nor will go see her right now. Because he's furious with her.

Because she's weak. Because she's a coward. Because she's a quitter. Because she wants to leave him and Jessie behind. Because she has put him in an impossible position. Because she's even considering taking that way out. Because she has asked for his blessing to do it.

Because he perhaps should have given it to her.

He gets up from the armchair, brings his coffee cup to the window, and drinks a few sips of it as he gazes out over town.

It seems unreal to him. Like a movie set that has never housed any real life. As if all those bright, yellow squares in the walls of houses out there in the night would be just that.

Yellow squares that would contain nothing but a small, glowing bulb if you got close enough to look inside.

That's how it feels here, in the living room where he's standing. Like a place that has never housed any real life.

He knows it's a lie. He knows it was a happy home four years ago. Christ, he can't even count the number of times he has stopped in the doorway because he spotted Michelle reading a book on this very windowsill, only to sneak up on her and kiss her neck.

These days, it's only Nathan's coffee cup that sits on the windowsill, as evidenced by the five Olympic rings in shades of brown on its surface.

How can she ask this of him? What would he even say to Jessie? Sorry, sweetie, your mom is not here anymore. I gave her permission to take her own life. Surely, you understand that, don't you?

He sighs, turns away from the depressing view from the living room window, and walks back to the couch. It also sighs as he sits down in it and puts the coffee cup on the table.

Maybe it would be a good idea to turn on the TV. Find some trivial sitcom or action movie to get his mind off it all.

He reaches out and grabs the remote control from the armrest of the couch ... but once he has got it, he doesn't use it to turn on the TV. He just lets go of it so it drops down on the couch's seat cushion.

It's because of the stain. The small, bleached stain on the armrest under the spot where the remote control was.

He had forgotten all about it.

In many ways, it was this modest, peanut-shaped stain that instigated the avalanche of misery that has heaped tons of pitch-black snow upon him for the past four years.

Back then, it wasn't a light brown, bleached stain on the fabric. Back then, the stain was a deep, burgundy-red color, because it was the first time Michelle coughed up blood. And it was the subsequent visit to the doctor's office that started it all.

Since then, she has coughed up lots of blood. Buckets of it—all while the white coats on the sidelines have stopped talking about recovery and now only use words like 'life extension,' 'realistic time horizon,' and 'pain reduction.'

And still, Nathan demands that she keeps hoping.
Fuck.

DAY 6

CHAPTER 33

Nathan wakes up at dawn to the sound of Meredith's cough. It's a frail cough, full of rattling. The kind you hear in old people with severe pneumonia.

She catches him looking at her, and her coughing fit turns into a strained chuckle.

"Not yet," she says. "You won't get out of making me breakfast one last time."

She sounds strangely uplifted today, almost cheerful, which Nathan assumes must be due to one of two things: Either she's relieved after their conversation yesterday and looking forward to getting off the derailed train ... or the dehydration has finally driven her crazy.

Both are plausible explanations.

"Classic English breakfast?" he jokes. "Bacon,

eggs, sausages, and the works. How does that sound?"

"Nah, I'm more in the mood for something maritime. Crab, perhaps?"

"Let me see what I can do."

This exchange of lighthearted comments takes no more than a handful of seconds and is actually a load of nonsense as both of them know that their thirst has almost completely killed their want for food. Still, for Nathan, this little verbal ping-pong is a much-appreciated break from thoughts of dehydration and death.

Appreciated, but also short-lived, because a moment later the wind picks up, making the caves and crevices of the canyon behind them howl like a pack of wolves. And that's all it takes to kill the mood and throw him back into their harsh reality.

"That's how it sounded last night," Meredith says, rubbing her shoulders. "I sure hope it'll calm down during the morning."

Nathan looks out over the landscape that their journey will take them through today and nods thoughtfully. The first part is okay. It has rocks, vegetation, and ample opportunity to find shelter from the wind. The next part, on the other hand, is far more open. It consists primarily of sand dunes—and he can already see light brown clouds of sand dancing across the ground.

One thing at a time, he tells himself. *First of all, you make some breakfast for your daughter. Then you can worry about the weather forecast afterward.*

With his priorities set, he gets up, puts his blanket as an extra layer over Jessie, who is still asleep, and gently strokes her hair. Next, he finds himself a useful murder weapon—a medium-sized rock whose one end tapers, making it perfect for crushing a crab's shield—and goes hunting.

When he returns half an hour later, Jessie has woken up. She sits next to Meredith, adding small, dried leaves to a fire that looks about as tired and worn as her.

"Good morning, sprout," he says, and to his surprise, he receives a smile from her. Not a big and wide one, but a smile, nonetheless.

"Good morning, Dad. I'm helping Meredith make a fire."

"Yeah, I see that. That's good. And I've got the food."

He holds up this morning's catch—two medium-sized crabs and a small one—in front of him and shrugs.

"I know you're sick of crabs and probably don't feel very hungry, but—"

"It's fine, Dad. We need the energy. I understand that."

For some reason, hearing her say those words hits Nathan like a punch in his gut. Maybe because it's a very adult thing to say.

"That's ... um," he says, swallowing so a click sounds in his throat. "That's very mature of you, sweetie. Thank you for that."

Jessie tilts her head as she stares, a bit puzzled, at him—and suddenly she's back to being his little seven-year-old daughter. A pale Oliver Twist version of her, admittedly, with dark shadows under her eyes and cracked lips ... but still his little princess.

After breakfast, they pack up and embark on the trek of the day. Things are moving slow today. *Too* slow in Nathan's opinion, but there's not much he can do about it, given that it's because of the dehydration. It makes their legs unsteady and their movements heavy, as if they were wading through knee-high mud.

The wind doesn't exactly help either. It has only intensified during the morning, and when you're that exhausted, it takes energy just to keep upright. And then there's the sand, which more and more often swirls up around them, forcing them to shield their mouths and eyes.

Hour after hour goes by, and in the sky above, the

sun always seems to be one step ahead, causing its unsparing light to constantly hit them from the same angle, simultaneously blinding them and burning their skin.

Every step is a challenge, every spot of shade a temptation, but Nathan is determined to hold his own reigns. When he is going to rest the next time, it will be on *his* terms. Because *he* chooses to, and not because the sun or the wind forces them to. No matter what tantrums the weather gods decide to throw.

Part of him is aware of the irrational, almost childish, nature of that logic, and he also realizes that he is thinking less clearly due to dehydration. Still, he stubbornly clings to the thought and uses it to push himself—and his two fellow travelers—to keep putting one foot in front of the other.

However, a moment arrives when he halts unexpectedly, without it being a deliberate decision. This happens around midday, right after having climbed to the peak of a sand dune. When preparing to descend on the other side, it catches his eye, and he gestures for the others to stop.

A flash of light. But not directly from the sun. A reflection.

"What's wrong, Dad?"

Nathan brushes her off with a movement of his

hand, simultaneously squinting his eyes and staring in the direction of the flash.

There it is again—and this time he's one hundred percent sure. Something out there catches the light of the sun and throws it in his direction. Something located at ground level.

"Nathan," Meredith says in a trembling almost gasping voice. "Is that ...?"

Her voice dies out before the sentence is finished, but Nathan has seen the same thing as her, and he knows she must have reached the same conclusion.

Somewhere out there in the barren desert, something is reflecting the sun's light, and it even seems to be surrounded by vegetation.

Did they just stumble upon a fucking oasis?

CHAPTER 34

His lungs contract in protest, streaks of pain shoot through the muscles of his legs, threatening to cause a cramp, and red sparks appear all over his field of vision.

Still, Nathan doesn't slow down. He staggers across the sand, swaying uncertainly from side to side like a man in the last stage of a drinking spree, but with his eyes on the prize. On the oasis and the flickering glimpses of the water reflecting the sun's light among the green vegetation.

He can almost taste it. Feel how it will alleviate his chapped lips. How it will tickle on his tongue. How his—

"Ow, Dad," sounds from behind him. "My hand. I can't keep up. It hurts."

Confused—and for a split second, annoyed—Nathan looks back, first at Jessie's face, then down at her hand, which he's holding. Then he blinks as if he has been torn out of a deep sleep.

"I'm sorry, sweetie," he croaks in a voice that feels hoarser and rougher than ever before. As if it hasn't been in use for years. "I'll slow down, okay?"

Jessie nods, but there's something about the way she looks at him. As if she doesn't quite trust that he will—or maybe *can*—keep that promise. It wouldn't be fair to blame her for that, though. He himself isn't entirely convinced.

For the same reason, he steps aside and invites Meredith and Jessie to take the lead so they can set the pace while he simply follows suit.

And as he takes his place there, a few yards behind his two fellow travelers, he suddenly realizes how battered and worn they actually look. It's the way they move. Hunched over, hands on their thighs, as if afraid that their upper bodies will tip over and break off at the hip if they don't apply counter pressure. They look ancient. Even Jessie.

As if they were targets of a prank from a god of bad taste, the wind picks up further as they approach the oasis. It whirls up large clouds of sand in front of them like it's trying to erase the miracle before they have a chance to reach it.

On the other hand, the wind might be trying to spare them. To protect them from the fateful realization that awaits them the minute it settles down again.

If so, it fails.

"No! No, no, no! That can't be right."

In his head, he shouts those words, roars them out like a furious war cry, but what actually comes out is a monotonous, half-choked murmur.

There *is* no miracle. The oasis isn't an oasis. There is a large, green plant growth, yes ... but it isn't a pool of water that reflected the sunlight. It's the glass in the cockpit window of the plane wreck on which the plants grow.

As a sad testimony to another time, the small transport plane lies abandoned here, in the middle of this desolate and secluded backdrop. Its hull is battered and covered in rust, its wings are bent, the engine intake is filled with plants, rock shards, and sand, and the propeller blades appear to be locked in their final position.

A thin coating of moss-like algae covers a large portion of the hull, while the surrounding area is blanketed with tall seagrass, the dry leaves of which rustle in the wind with an unnerving, whispering sound.

The weight of defeat hits Nathan, falls like a

heavy sandbag on his shoulders, and threatens to bring him to his knees.

He looks at Jessie and opens his mouth to tell her that he's sorry. That he's ashamed of having been so naive that he allowed himself to hope. That he allowed *her* to hope.

He never gets to say any of these things, though, because behind Jessie's back, Meredith stands—and when he sees her face, he loses his voice.

Meredith doesn't look disheartened. In fact, her eyes carry some of the same peculiar cheerfulness that she had when they got up this morning.

"Are you ... okay, Meredith?"

She looks at him, then at the plane wreck, and then back at him.

"It's a sign," she says, shaking her hands as if she is barely able to contain her excitement. "Don't you see it?"

Out of the corner of his eye, he sees Jessie take a few steps backward. Maybe it's just a coincidence, but he doesn't think so. He's pretty sure that Jessie— like him—is a bit daunted by Meredith's behavior right now. By the high-pitched undertone of her voice and the intense look in her eyes.

"You really don't see it?" she asks again.

"See what?"

"That it's a sign. Don't you remember what we talked about last night? I told you about ..."

She hesitates and squints down at Jessie, the way adults do when the topic of conversation is entering non-child-friendly territory.

"About George," she finishes, half in a whisper. "My husband, who, um ... who didn't like to travel."

"Meredith, I'm not sure I'm following you, but—"

Suddenly, he is. Suddenly, the whole context is so clear to him that it might as well have been written on a giant neon sign out here.

Maybe a year up in Heaven has cured his fear of heights, so I can finally get him on a plane. Go for an adventure.

That's how Meredith put it last night. And now they're standing here, smack dab in front of the wreckage of an airplane. You can hardly blame her for jumping to the conclusion that it's a sign. Especially not when you factor in the enormous amount of psychological pressure she has been under.

He turns to Jessie and gives her a *wait here a moment* message with his hand. Then he walks over to Meredith and places a hand gently on her upper arm, saying in a hushed voice:

"I get why you would think it must be a sign, but ... I promise you, it's a coincidence."

She puts her skinny old hand over his and gives him a strangely sympathetic smile.

"You're free to believe whatever you want," she whispers, calmly and without judgment. "But I feel it, deep in my heart, that this is where my journey ends. This is where I say goodbye."

"But ..." Nathan says, turning his head to look at Jessie, but immediately Meredith grabs his arm and forces his gaze back on her.

"And you *promised* me, Nathan. You promised it wouldn't become a big deal."

Nathan stares at her, fiercely and for a long time, while biting his lower lip. Then his gaze falls to the ground, and he sighs.

"When?"

"When you move on, I'll stay behind."

"I don't know if Jessie can handle—"

"Jessie doesn't need to know more than she needs to know," Meredith interrupts, moving her hand up to his shoulder. "Does she?"

Another long pause, during which Nathan simply stares at her, followed by another deep sigh.

"No, I guess she doesn't."

"Good," Meredith says, winking at him. "Now, shouldn't we take a closer look at that plane instead of standing here, chatting the day away? If we're lucky, there might be something good on board."

CHAPTER 35

The hinges squeal and thin flakes of rust sprinkle down as Nathan pulls open the cockpit door. Since the only light comes from a few areas of the cockpit window that aren't covered by algae growth, the inside is dark, and he hesitates for a moment to allow his eyes to adjust before fully entering.

Even in this scarce lighting, the chaos is obvious. The dashboard is torn loose and shattered, leaving metal parts, wires, and glass shards sticking out all over the place. All of them corroded and covered in rust and dirt.

From the dashboard, Nathan's gaze moves over to the pilot's seat, which has been pulled free of its anchor rail and now leans crookedly to one side. Its dirty, cracked leather cover carries a nauseating smell of stale humidity that has had years to settle in.

There is no trace of the pilot. If he was in the cockpit when the plane crashed, that's no longer the case—which is the first check mark on Nathan's list before calling the others in. That there are no creepy, uniformed skeletons—nor bloodthirsty lobster monsters—to be found in the cockpit.

So far, so good.

He turns around, opens a sliding door, and enters the cargo compartment, which is quite a disappointment. Firstly, there are only five boxes stacked up in there, and secondly, they are made of cardboard, which means that they are so dissolved that the stack mostly looks like a large, clumsy tower of modeling clay, held up only by the freight belts in the wall.

The third—and biggest—disappointment is the contents of the boxes. For whatever the crumbling substances once were, one thing is certain: it wasn't food.

"You're okay to come in here, girls!"

"Oh, it doesn't exactly smell like roses, huh?" he hears Meredith say from inside the cockpit shortly after.

He doesn't answer, because her tone of voice—a bit too chirpy for the circumstances—reveals that he's not the one she's talking to.

"No," Jessie replies. "It's ... a bit scary."

"I'm in here, sweetie," Nathan says as he bends down and opens some small hatches lined up under a little, two-seat bench on the left side of the cargo compartment. "You can come in here if you want."

Behind the hatches, there isn't much to come by either. Two inflatable life jackets and a box of batteries and small bulbs rusted together into one large lump. Not exactly worth writing home about.

He hears a sound behind him and turns around. It's Jessie. She stands quietly in the doorway, her gaze wandering from corner to corner in the cargo compartment.

In the background behind her, he can see Meredith. She is standing with her back to them, apparently studying the crooked pilot's seat.

"Come on in, sweetie," Nathan says. "You can help me look."

Jessie carefully steps into the room, and as she walks over to him, he notices that she remains close to the side wall so she can lean on it. He'd like to think it was because of the plane's floor sloping downward, but he's pretty sure the explanation lies in her depleted body.

When she has come all the way over to him, he strokes a hand lovingly over her hair, then nods toward an electronic panel that sits on the wall next to the tower of disintegrated boxes on the opposite side. Presumably, it was used for monitoring things like temperature and pressure in the cargo compartment, but like the instruments in the cockpit, this panel is also broken.

That detail doesn't worry him, though, because it's the small locker above it that has caught his interest. Especially the red plastic box he can make out behind the half-open door.

"Should we try checking up there?"

Jessie nods and follows him over there, even though her eyes reveal that she harbors little hope for success.

He tries to keep his cool, especially after being wrong about the oasis, but still, he can't help but smile when he sees the first-aid symbol on the lid of the box.

With trembling fingers and bated breath, he grabs and twists the tight, gear-like locking mechanisms that keep the rubber edge of the lid pressed against the box, keeping it waterproof.

The lock clicks one, two, three, four times, after which the lid pops up with a hiss, and the contents are exposed.

Basic first-aid tools, a flashlight, some painkillers, a utility knife, and ...

"Is this a joke?" Nathan sneers, not knowing

whom the question is aimed at. "Water purification tablets? A fucking pack of *water purification tablets*?"

That discovery makes him so angry that he nearly slams the lid shut and throws the first-aid kit away before he has a chance to see what's hiding under the tablets.

However, his eyes do catch sight of it. A little can, filled with liquid.

Not water, but the next best thing.

"Meredith?" Nathan calls, exchanging a smile with Jessie. "Come in here for a second."

"What's the matter?"

Nathan answers her by raising his hand and showing her the can.

"I'd like to invite you to dinner tonight. We're having potato soup."

From the doorway, Meredith studies the can, though not quite with the enthusiasm he had expected to see.

"That's very nice of you," she says, smiling. "But I've made other plans, remember?"

Yeah, but there's no harm in trying, is there? Nathan thinks as he nods and slowly lowers his hand again.

"What is she talking about?" Jessie asks uncertainly, though her voice—and the fact that she's directing the question at him rather than at Meredith—suggests that she might already know.

"My old legs are tired," Meredith explains, still smiling and still with an almost stoic calm in her voice. "They can't keep walking. That's why your father and I have agreed that I'll stay behind when you move on."

Nathan feels the weight of Jessie's questioning gaze as it moves onto him, and he can barely take it as he answers her with a nod.

"But don't worry," Meredith continues. "Obviously, the plan is for you to come back and get me when you've found help."

Jessie squints her eyes and starts to turn her head from side to side, slowly at first, then faster and faster.

"I want to stay here too," she says. "Can't we stay here?"

Nathan crouches down, takes her in his arms, and hugs her.

"We can't, sweetie," he whispers. "We have to keep going ... and we need to be strong. *You* need to be strong, for Meredith's sake and for mine."

No answer, only a faint sobbing against his chest.

"I need you to be as brave as Astronaut Bray, as clever as Captain Jolly, and as strong as Miss Jawbreaker, okay? But most of all, I need Jessie. Because what are you?"

"Your butt-kicking daughter," Jessie whispers reluctantly, and Nathan hugs her even harder.

"That's right. My awe-inspiring, butt-kicking daughter who can handle anything."

For a long time, Nathan stays that way, with Jessie wrapped in his arms and her head resting on his chest while he listens to the sound of her breathing —and only when it's completely calm does he loosen his embrace.

When she lifts her head again, there is a noticeable change in Jessie's face. She's clearly still sad, but her eyes look serious.

"How long can we stay?" she asks.

"Not long, I'm afraid," he replies, grimacing. "We can take a short break, but then we have to move on. Five minutes. Maybe ten."

Jessie purses her lips together and lets out a sigh. Then she nods to herself, walks over to Meredith, and takes her by the hand. Afterward, without exchanging a word, the two of them walk over to the pilot's seat and sit down. Meredith on the seat, Jessie on her lap.

There they stay while Nathan searches the rest of the plane wreckage. What they're whispering about during that time, he has no idea, nor is he going to ask. What's important to him is that the parting doesn't crush Jessie—and that doesn't seem to be the case. At least she neither protests nor breaks down when, a while later, he puts his hand on her shoulder and gives her the *it's time* nod. She just gives Meredith one last hug and then walks to the doorway to wait for him.

His own goodbye to Meredith is also relatively undramatic. He asks her if she's sure. She answers yes. He asks her if she doesn't at least want one of the blankets from the bag. She answers no. He asks her if she's sure. She answers yes again. He wishes her a good journey and tells her to say hi to George. She says thank you and that she will. He takes her hand, holds it for a while, and gives it one last squeeze. He then turns around and leaves the cockpit, while Meredith remains seated in the pilot's seat, reclined and with a hint of a smile on her lips.

"Now it's just the two of us," Nathan says, as cheerfully as he can, as he comes out to Jessie. "What do you say we put on our spacesuits again and find that sea turtle?"

Jessie stares at him with a facial expression that he finds hard to read because she looks so bushed with her chapped lips, her sunken eyes, and her drowsy, almost feverish gaze. Only when she raises her hands and puts on her invisible space helmet does her answer become clear to him.

He copies the movement, and when he, too, has his helmet clicked into place, he holds out his hand.

Jessie takes it, and then they head out together into the harsh landscape, where the increasing wind is well on its way to becoming an outright storm that —like a mean kid on a playground—hurls larger and larger handfuls of sand into the air.

CHAPTER 36

Is the sky above them still blue? Nathan has no idea, because the sky, like everything else, has disappeared behind the sandy mist swirling around them. Swallowed by the chaos of sand grains that try to sneak into their eyes and sting their skin like needles. Every gust of wind seems to steal more moisture from their parched bodies, every strained breath is filled with the grainy taste of the sand, and behind them, every footprint is wiped out so it's like they've never been there.

The sandstorm is merciless. Still, they go on. Two dusty wanderers whose intertwined fingers are the only anchor in a world that no longer welcomes them and can no longer cover their most basic needs.

Like the sky and footprints, their end goal has

also been blurred out. Lashed to pieces by the storm's unrelenting onslaught and reduced to three simple words:

One more step.

He has said those exact words several times to Jessie during the afternoon, back when they could still talk without getting their tongues coated with sand dust. Now they only speak if it's absolutely necessary, and the three words are now forced to stay in the back of Nathan's mind as he rapidly approaches the point where his legs can no longer carry him.

Jessie is almost there already. Twice she has collapsed on the sand because her legs gave way under her without warning.

The first time she got up again on her own. The second time Nathan had to help her. He isn't sure he has the strength to do so if there is a third.

One more step.

He's worried about her. About her tiny, seven-year-old body, which craves water so much that he regularly sees her run a parched tongue over her chapped lips. But the only liquid it can hope to find there is a drop of blood or two from the small wounds that have appeared in the corners of her mouth.

Just one more step.

His own thirst is also agonizing. It's there constantly, like a noose around his neck that tightens each time he swallows. Or *tries* to swallow. He also has a migraine. One of the bad ones. The kind that makes you dizzy and causes your vision to flutter unsteadily.

Oh yes, there's plenty wrong with him as well, and if they don't find shelter from the wind soon, it may well be—

A strong burst of wind rips this thought—as well as his foothold—from him, and within a second, his eyes are forced shut while his mouth and nostrils are filled with grains of sand.

He tries to cough it out but can't. Tries again, with no luck. Tries a third time and ... oh God, he manages to get enough out to get some air in.

He presses his hands down into the sand and pushes until he's up far enough to pull his knees up under him and rest on them. Then he lifts his head ... and stiffens.

A hallucination, that's all. He knows this just as surely as he knows that the sun is warm and that he loves his daughter.

But it's right there, on the other side of the sandstorm's brown barrier; a hazy collection of towers and spires hovering like an optical illusion above the dreary, parched seafloor's horizon line. A breathtaking castle.

Something in him protests:

It's not a castle. It's the Mansion of Mirrors.

Without being able to explain why, he instinctively knows that this indeed is the true name of the gray-black building with the tall towers out there. The Mansion of Mirrors.

Is that where we're headed?

Hardly has he finished that thought before the mansion starts to disappear. It dissolves as if it were built of the same sand that surrounds him. In its place, something new emerges. A blurred entity that gets closer and closer as it slowly takes shape.

He jolts as two small, white hands suddenly manifest in front of it and grab his arm.

"Get up, Dad," he hears Jessie say in a voice that —even though she's standing right in front of him— sounds like it's coming from far away. "Please, I need you."

Her hair flutters wildly around her face, and behind it, he can see her eyes narrowing from the exertion as she pulls on his arm to get him up.

He can see it, yes. But she's so weak that he can hardly feel it.

After two more unsuccessful attempts, the last strength runs out of the girl like water in a dark drain. She lets go of his arm, sinks to her knees, and tumbles helplessly toward him.

Somehow, he finds the strength to grab her—and somehow, he finds the strength to stand up with her limp body hanging over his shoulder as he takes a step forward.

And then one more.

And one more.

Just ... one ... more ... step.

He continues like this, stubbornly ignoring the cries of pain from the muscles of his exhausted body and the voice of the wind telling him in a seductive whisper that it's okay for him to lie down again. That there would be no harm in taking a well-deserved rest.

He doesn't even have a direction anymore. Every time he tries to find his bearings, he's met by rolling sandbanks and tilted, shuddering horizons. His internal compass is worthless, and his eyes are no longer able to read the exterior one.

The sand and wind have rendered all his senses useless and left him at the mercy of the goddess of fate, who slowly and heartlessly drowns him in this roaring, light-brown sea.

Until she—completely unexpected and perhaps out of boredom—changes her mind and throws him a rope.

All of a sudden, they're there, as if summoned with a magical flick of the wrist. A large arch with white pillars, leaning down over him from both sides, offering a temporary shelter.

With one last effort, he staggers to the largest of the pillars, where, still with Jessie in his arms, he falls to his knees and crawls into a crescent-shaped notch just big enough to house them both and shield them from the worst of the sandstorm's fury.

And lying there, darkness finally catches up with Nathan.

CHAPTER 37

In the end, Nathan couldn't do it. He couldn't sit down, take her hand in his, and give her his blessing.

And now it's too late. His wife—whose name is engraved on the tombstone he sits in front of—has left the world of the living, and he couldn't find it in him to let her do it on her own terms.

Because of him, Michelle's parting with life wasn't graceful. It was prolonged and filled with suffering. She died in a body so consumed by illness that it was like looking at a complete stranger. A gray-skinned old lady who by the end was so hollow and withered that you could hardly make out the contours of her body as it lay under the blanket in the hospital bed.

Unworthy. That's what it was.

And yet he couldn't bring himself to let her take the other way out. Because he thought it was the easy one.

He's no longer so sure of that.

"Your parents took Jessie to Marine World yesterday," he whispers into the empty air above the gravesite. *"She was buzzing when she came home, and she couldn't stop talking about it. I almost got a full lecture on sea turtles before she talked herself to sleep on the couch."*

A faint breeze makes the trees whisper behind his back as if they're agreeing on how strange he is, sitting and talking to himself like that.

"They've been great, your parents," he continues. *"They have their own grief to struggle with, and yet they have been amazing grandparents to her. I'm really thankful for the way they're always there for us. I ..."*

He feels his throat constrict and has to take a moment before he's able to continue.

"I'm really trying to create a stable everyday life for Jessie. We cook her favorite meals, read books together, and go over to the playground in the park all the time. But it's hard, Michelle. So hard. She ... she asked me the other day why you're not with us anymore. It was so hard to explain to her that you're in our hearts, but not ..."

Now the tears can't be held back any longer. They stream down Nathan's cheeks, meet on his chin, and from there drip onto the grass.

The gravesite is green and well-kept, and the entire

cemetery smells of fresh flowers. At this time of day, when the sun is high in the sky and gives everything a warm, orange glow, it's a beautiful place.

A stark contrast to the gloomy and godforsaken wasteland inside of Nathan.

"She looked at me with, um ... with your eyes and said she misses her mom," he stammers before emotions over-power him again and close up his throat.

Only this time it isn't caused by grief, but by shame.

It's the images that pop into his head that trigger it. Their identical eyes.

Jessie's eyes as she said she missed her mother.

Michelle's eyes, just before they closed for the final time, and the insufferable pain that was the last six months of her life finally came to an end.

A pain that he could have spared her if only he had been strong enough.

Still with his wife's blue irises imprinted on the inside of his eyelids, Nathan folds his hands, lets his head fall forward ... and begs for her forgiveness.

DAY 7

CHAPTER 38

The calm after the storm. That must be the most appropriate description of what meets Nathan when he wakes up with a gasp and opens his eyes the next morning.

Quiet and struck with almost religious awe, he lets his gaze wander over the pillars of the protective arch that manifested itself amidst the withered landscape and saved him. Except that these aren't pillars that some merciful god has arisen for their sake. They are ribs in the skeleton of a giant sea creature, shiny and glistening from the sand that has swirled around them.

From the night's sanctuary, his gaze glides out to the landscape on the other side. Last night it was the courtyard of Hell, where only chaos and destruction reigned. This morning, a deep, almost harmonious calm rests over the barren, desert-like seabed. As if it, in the aftermath of its violent rebellion, has finally accepted its fate.

Something similar could be said about Nathan. Perhaps that's why, despite the rapid and inevitable decay of his aching body, he's able to see the beauty of the sand now. To appreciate the dunes that look like frozen waves in a vast, bright brown ocean, while thousands of tiny grains of sand shimmer in them like freshly fallen snow under the light of the morning sun.

A gentle gust of wind caresses his cheeks, and he closes his eyes as he takes a breath. It still stings in his dry throat, but the air is fresh and cold and carries with it a hint of salt that further awakens his senses. Wrestles him free of ...

One more step.

"Jessie?" he croaks out through his cracked lips as he struggles up into a sitting position. "Jessie, where are you?"

Suddenly, it's difficult for him to focus again. As if all the sand dust from yesterday is back in his eyes, making them sting.

He puts his hands in the sand, pushes himself up —and falls down. He tries again, this time using one of the large rib bones for support, and it proves more effective. He's still not stable on his legs, far from it, but he's up and he can move ... if he just makes sure to take it easy.

Out of the corner of his eye, he sees the emergency bag lying on the ground, and a terrible thought shoots into him:

What if Jessie isn't here at all? What if his dehydrated brain just made him *think* that he was carrying her with him?

One more step.

What if it was just the emergency bag he was lugging around? If that was what he was holding in his arms?

No, it was Jessie, he thinks, frantically looking around, hoping to find some confirmation.

A relief, deep and intense, courses through his body as he sees it. A blend of small footprints and wide tracks, as if someone has alternately walked and crawled across the sand—and they lead out of the bone arch on the opposite side of where he entered last night.

Stumbling uncertainly, he follows the trail that leads him out between two of the skeleton's large, pearly-white ribs, past a dried-out, yellowish seaweed plant, and from there down a sand dune, glimmering like gold in the sun.

She sits at the foot of it, hunched over with her

legs crossed, staring out over the sand. She has her back to him, and her upper body is swaying slightly from side to side, as if she's rocking to the beat of a slow piece of music.

As he approaches, he can hear her too. Whether it's an actual melody or just a series of random notes is impossible to determine, since her voice is muffled and hoarse, but that she is humming something is for certain.

She must have sensed his presence because now she turns her face and looks at him with eyes that are feverish and glassy.

"We did it, Dad," she says, spreading her pale, chapped lips in a smile that makes a chill run down Nathan's spine. "We found it."

She stares at him, waiting for a reaction or an answer, but Nathan is so paralyzed that he can't give her either.

She looks wrecked. No, more than that. She looks *ill*. Seriously ill. Her skin is porcelain white and shiny, her cheeks sunken so that the cheekbones protrude. Above them lie two deep circles, dark as coal, beneath the eyes.

And still, her lips carry that creepy smile.

"What did we find, sweetie?" he manages to get out.

Instead of answering with words, Jessie raises her

hand and points out to the sand with a finger that shakes slightly, as if it's only partly under her control.

Nathan follows the direction ... and sees nothing but golden-brown sand.

"You can't see it?" Jessie asks. "It's right there."

Nathan squints his eyes and lets his gaze wander, first from side to side, then across the dunes, all the way to the horizon and back.

And then, following a brief visit to the blue sky that no longer houses any clouds, he suddenly sees it, wandering across the sand with slow, considered steps.

"I see it," he whispers, sitting down on the sand next to Jessie. "Have you given it a name yet?"

A moment of reflection. Then Jessie nods to herself.

"Tommy, maybe?"

"Tommy?" Nathan repeats, tasting the word. "Like the boy from the letter? I like that. It's a good name for a sea turtle."

Those words are followed by another long pause, during which father and daughter do nothing but sit completely silent while studying the fascinating animal.

Although here in the dune fields it's probably more of a burden than a shield, its shell is impressive. A dome-shaped armor that for decades, maybe even centuries, has protected the turtle from the dangers of the sea—and which has the story of each encounter with these engraved in its rough surface.

But it isn't just the shell's scratches and cracks that tell of the sea turtle's long life, for its dark, watchful eyes look as if they carry countless secrets from the farthest corners and deepest abysses of the world.

Tommy the sea turtle. Nathan could sit here forever, just staring at him ... but he knows it's out of the question. That there is something he needs to take care of.

"Well, I'd better get to work," he says, patting himself on the thighs. "Breakfast won't make itself."

Jessie nods but continues to stare absentmindedly into the sand, not bothering to look at him. He's about to touch her shoulder to get her attention but then stops himself and withdraws his hand.

"I'll ... be back in a bit, okay?"

With those words, he pushes himself up and staggers back to the weathered, yellowish seaweed he passed on his way out of the bone arch. From the plant, he picks a few handfuls of dry leaves, planning to use them to make a campfire.

And yes, he does realize that this project will cost everything his worn-out body has left to give, but it's a price he's willing to pay. A price he *has* to pay if he plans to serve his daughter a warm breakfast.

And that *is* his plan. The only one he has left.

With the dry leaves in his hands, he continues on his shaky legs until he is inside the bone arch, where he drops down onto his knees next to the emergency bag and starts preparing the fire.

He begins by taking two of the blankets from the bag and rolling them up as tightly as his sore muscles allow until they are shaped like two small, firm clubs. Next, he digs a hole in the sand and lays the two blanket rolls in a cross at the bottom. They are not as optimal as two pieces of wood would have been, but they should be able to burn long enough for his purpose.

With the foundation of the fire in place, it's time to add kindling. In this case, it's the dry seaweed leaves that he now starts to tear into smaller pieces, after which he arranges them below, and in a circle around, the blanket rolls. When this is done, he takes the storm lighter from the bag, lights it, and moves the flame to the leaves.

A faint crackling sound emerges as the fire takes hold of the dry leaves and then spreads to the blanket rolls.

The final component is the can of potato soup that they found in the plane wreckage. He opens it,

PER JACOBSEN

places it carefully in the middle of the fire, and then he waits ... which is no easy task, given how tired he is by now.

Fifteen minutes later, small bubbles start emerging on the surface of the soup, but Nathan doesn't take it off the heat right away. Instead, he opens the emergency bag one last time, pulls out the wine bottle, and gently swirls it while studying its contents.

About a quarter of an inch of the bottom of the bottle is covered. More than enough.

Carefully, he tips the bottle and pours all of it into the soup. Then he pulls out the Swiss Army knife, cleans its blade with the fire, and uses it to stir the soup until all visible traces of the viscous, green liquid are gone.

With his folded jacket as protection for his hands, he carries the can of hot soup out of the bone arch and down the sand dune. Down to Jessie.

"Breakfast is served, sprout," he says, handing her the can.

Jessie nods and accepts it but says nothing. She doesn't even scold him for calling her sprout. But that's okay. It would only have made it harder.

He takes a seat in the sand next to her and gently strokes a hand over her back.

"You better eat it while it's hot."

For a little while, she just sits there, holding the can in front of her chest without doing anything. Then her feverish eyes blink as if his words have only just reached her, and she puffs on the soup.

Nathan watches her in tense silence as she brings the can to her mouth, and only after watching her take a few sips—and swallow them—is he able to breathe again.

She hands the can back to him, and as he accepts it, he nods toward the sandbank in front of them.

"He isn't exactly in a hurry, huh? Where do you think he's going?"

Jessie looks out there with feverish eyes that flicker up and down, finding no anchoring point.

"Home," she then says. "Like us."

AFTERWORD

What kind of bizarre way to end a story is that? What the heck is wrong with that author?

Should you be left with one of these questions—or perhaps both—after reading the last page of the story, I don't blame you. But please, allow me to try to explain before you close the book and never again open one with my name on the cover.

Is there meaning behind the madness? Yes, I believe there is. You see, I've always been an advocate for talking openly about all of life's matters—even the more difficult ones like death, illness, depression, and suicide. As a result, those darker topics always seem to find a way into my stories. However, with *Dry*, it was a conscious decision as I was curious to see what would happen if I forced my characters to deal with some of the worst imaginable versions of these dark topics. I guess you could say that I used their actions as a mouthpiece as well as a tool for examining my own beliefs.

It didn't take long before I realized that I really had something on my mind. So far, *Dry* is the book that I have written in the shortest time (two months), and it came to me as an almost fully developed idea. I saw the events clearly; I knew it had to play out over seven days and that it had to end in the oddly 'Shakespearian' way that it did. And I knew it was going to be about a father who has to make the hardest decision ever.

The side story—the nights where we travel back to Michelle's illness—also came to me pretty quickly as I realized I needed to explain *how* Nathan was able to make the final decision.

Because I'm a father myself, a soft one at that, and I know that it would take far more than just the perception that it's the right decision. Therefore, I gave Nathan some help in making the choice by giving him a past where he saw what the opposite decision cost him—and especially his wife.

My hope is that Nathan's final decision, whether you agree with it or not, will provoke some thoughts and maybe even inspire you to have a chat with your loved ones about some of life's heavier topics.

Well, I think that was it. All that remains is to say thank you to the wonderful people who have helped me get this book across the finish line so quickly. They are *Sarah Jacobsen*, my eternal first reader and co-conspirator in this life, and *Kaare* & *Karina Bertelsen Dantoft*, my dynamic beta reader duo.

Last—but never least—I owe the usual thanks to you, dear reader. Our time is valuable, and I'm honored that you decided to spend some of yours reading my words.

— PER JACOBSEN

Printed in Great Britain
by Amazon